Walter Arnold

The Life and Death of the Sublime Society of Beef Steaks

Walter Arnold

The Life and Death of the Sublime Society of Beef Steaks

ISBN/EAN: 9783337056100

Printed in Europe, USA, Canada, Australia, Japan

Cover: Foto ©Raphael Reischuk / pixelio.de

More available books at **www.hansebooks.com**

THE

LIFE AND DEATH

OF THE

Sublime Society of Beef Steaks.

BY

Bro. WALTER ARNOLD.

" What a host of bright names to our memories dear
In its magical circle enchanted appear,
Crowding round the old bar that once furnished their cheer
To the jolly old Steakers of England."
Anthem.

LONDON:

BRADBURY, EVANS, & CO., 10, BOUVERIE STREET, E.C.

1871.

TO BROTHER

THE DUKE OF LEINSTER,

WHO AT THE TIME OF ITS DISSOLUTION HAD BEEN FOR 45 YEARS

A MEMBER OF

The Sublime Society of Beef Steaks,

This Volume is Dedicated,

IN AFFECTIONATE REMEMBRANCE, BY ITS COMPILER,

WALTER ARNOLD.

CONTENTS.

LIST OF ILLUSTRATIONS.

The Compiler is indebted to Sir AUBREY PAUL, Bart., for the Photograph of the President's Chair, and to Major GRESLEY for the remainder.

THE

ORIGINAL TWENTY-FOUR MEMBERS OF THE SUBLIME SOCIETY OF BEEF STEAKS,

FOUNDED IN THE YEAR 1735 BY JOHN RICH,

HARLEQUIN AND MACHINIST AT COVENT GARDEN.

" First Rich who this feast of the gridiron planned,
And formed with a touch of his harlequin's wand
Out of mighty rude matter this brotherly band,
The jolly old Steakers of England."

Anthem.

JOHN RICH (the Founder).

GEORGE LAMBERT.

WILLIAM HOGARTH.

LACY RYAN.

EBENEZER FORREST.

ROBERT SCOTT.

THOMAS CHAPMAN.

DENNIS DELANE.

JOHN THORNHILL.

FRANCIS NIVELON.

SIR WILLIAM SAUNDERSON.

JOHN MITCHELL.

THOMAS BOSON.

HENRY SMART.

HUGH WATSON.

WILLIAM WATSON.

WILLIAM HUGGINS.

EDWARD TUFFNELL.

THOMAS SALWAY.

CHARLES NEALE.

CHARLES LATOUZE.

ALEXANDER GORDON.

WILLIAM TOTHALL.

GABRIEL HUNT.

THE

RULES OF THE SUBLIME SOCIETY OF BEEF STEAKS.

JANUARY 11TH, 1735.

Resolved and Ordered:—That all the Laws and Orders at any time heretofore made in this Society be now repealed and made void, and that none of the following Laws or Orders, or any other Laws or Orders that shall be hereafter made, shall be repealed or made void, or in any manner varied, unless moved for and seconded at one Meeting, and voted by the majority and ordered at the next Meeting of this Society.

1. That the Members of this Society shall not exceed twenty-four in number.

2. That whenever any Member's seat shall be declared

vacant, every Member present then or on the two succeeding days of Meeting may propose a person (not present) to fill up such vacancy, and on the third day of Meeting after such vacancy declared, the Members then present shall proceed to the election of a person to supply the same (by balloting), and the person for whom the majority shall be, shall be declared duly elected a Member of this Society, and on his admission shall pay three guineas to the Treasurer for the use of this Society.

3. That every Member shall succeed in rotation to the dignity of President, and on that day bear the expense of the Beef, and, if then present, may introduce one person as a visitor without incurring any penalty for so doing, and if absent, the last President then present shall officiate (in his stead) as President of this Society.

4. That Beef Steaks shall be the only meat for dinner, and the broiling begin at two of the clock on each day of Meeting, and the table-cloth be removed at half-an-hour after three.

5. That no Liquor after the first quantity shall be introduced, unless voted by the majority, and ordered before six of the clock in the evening.

6. That such Members who have quitted this Society (without being expelled) may be permitted to visit at any Meeting on paying equally with the Members then present.

7. That every Member who shall introduce any person or persons as a visitor or visitors at any day of Meeting (except as above mentioned), shall incur a penalty of five shillings for each person so introduced, to be paid to the Treasurer for the use of the Society. But on the first day of Meeting, and on the first Saturday in December, the first Saturday in February, and the last day of Meeting in each season, no visitors shall be admitted.

8. That if any Member shall propose to lay a wager in this Society, and the person to whom it shall be proposed shall ˙ accept the same by saying, Done, it shall be deemed a wager laid, whether the proposer does or does not reply to such

acceptance of his proposal, and whatever shall be lost on any wager laid in this Society shall be paid to the Treasurer for the use of this Society.

9. That the President for the time being shall be invested with the insignia, and order and decency be duly observed while the house is sitting, and more especially whenever the President shall call to order, and any motion being made and seconded, and not withdrawn, the question moved for shall (after free debate thereon) be put and determined before any other, except the previous question.

10. That every Member who shall be found guilty of any crime or misdemeanour in this Society, and shall neglect or refuse to submit to the penalty or censure by him incurred, and duly voted and ordered by the majority, and every member absenting himself three successive days of Meeting (unless excused for such absence by the majority), shall stand expelled this Society.

THE

SUCCESSORS OF THE ORIGINAL TWENTY-FOUR MEMBERS.

John Winde	February 12, 1736
Francis Mannock	November 17, 1736
John Elliott	November 27, 1736
Christopher Roberts	November 27, 1736
John George Cox	December 3, 1736
John Maitland	January 5, 1737
Charles Greenwood	November 12, 1737
Robert Winde	April 22, 1738
Charles Price	April 29, 1738
Joseph Porter	September 16, 1738
William D'ffesh	December 30, 1738
James Morris	January 19, 1739
J. K. Holtzmann	March 31, 1739
Theophilus Cibber	September 22, 1739
John Hippersley	October 23, 1739
Saunders Welsh	October 27, 1739
Charles Kirkmann	December 29, 1739
Christopher Serjeant	March 7, 1740
Sir H. Hicks	May 17, 1740
Isaac Ware	November 27, 1740

John George Cox . .	January 9,	1741
William Atkinson	February 5,	1741
Thomas Stephens	February 6,	1741
John Hodgson	May 16,	1741
Charles Gardiner	October 3,	1741
Henry Thelsall	October 16,	1741
William Hogarth (re-elected)	January 29,	1742
James Leake	March 28,	1742
Francis Haymann	February 5,	1742
Thomas Hundeeshagen	October 9,	1742
John Hayes	November 13,	1742
George Turner	May 7,	1743
Herbert Laurence	October 1,	1743
John Beard	December 24,	1743
Dennis Delane (re-elected) . . .	September 1,	1744
Paul Whitehead	October 20,	1744
Alexander Cruge	December 15,	1744
Henry Gifford	October 5,	1745
Thomas Wagg	October 5,	1745
William Ryley	November 16,	1745
William Howard	December 28,	1745
John Winde	January 14,	1746
John White	January 24,	1746
John Elliott	October 6,	1746
Robert Macky	February 18,	1748
Dr. W. Barrowby	December 3,	1748
James Bencraft	December 17,	1748
William Hollis	December 31,	1748
Alexander Forbes	February 19,	1749
Thomas Spencer	October 21,	1749
Anthony Askew, M.D.	May 5,	1750

Richard Grindall	October 26,	1750
Thomas Hudson	December 29,	1750
William Fogg	February 1,	1752
John Wilkes, M.P.	January 19,	1754
John Lidderdale	October 5,	1754
William Fitzherbert	January 21,	1758
Benjamin Read	April 15,	1758
John Catanack	February 10,	1759
Daniel Goatley	April 28,	1759
Alexander Reid	April 28,	1759
William Savage	October 13,	1759
Earl of Sandwich	Dec. 19,	1761
Samuel Darker	February 13,	1762
Josias Tarrer	February 20,	1762
Edward Bentham	May 8,	1762
Theodosius Forrest	January 22,	1763
Montague Lawrence	May 28,	1763
Earl of Effingham	March 31,	1764
John Webb	April 21,	1764
Robert Baldy	June 23,	1764
John Walton	February 16,	1765
Chace Price	March 6,	1765
Edward Bowman	February 8,	1766
George Colman	October 17,	1767
John Trevanion	February 18,	1769
Josiah Williamson	November 11,	1769
John Darker	November 18,	1769
Thomas Foley	April 28,	1770
Michael Adolphus	March 4,	1771
Thomas Harris	December 21,	1771
Earl of Surrey	February 22,	1772

John Churchill	February 29,	1772
Samuel Howard	March 8,	1772
James Leake	March 28,	1772
Colonel W. Miles	February 12,	1774
Michael Bourne	November 12,	1774
William Ellis	November 19,	1774
William Nettleship	December 12,	1775
Sir Harry Inglefield	November 29,	1776
Earl of Inchquin	November 22,	1777
Sir J. Lovett	February 22,	1778
Duke of Norfolk	January 16,	1779
P. Rosenhagen	February 5,	1780
H. Fendall	February 12,	1780
Sir J. Boyd	February 26,	1780
Samuel Johnson	March 4,	1780
J. Walton	November 21,	1781
Earl of Effingham	March 16,	1782
Michael Hare	March 23,	1782
Thomas King	February 22,	1783
G. Colman	January 24,	1784
Wilson Braddyll	March 13,	1784
Earl of Guilford	March 13,	1784
Charles Morris	February 12,	1785
H. R. H. the Prince of Wales	May 7,	1785
Barrington Bradshaw	November 25,	1785
James Cobb	February 11,	1786
Sir Michael Nugent	November 25,	1786
H. R. H. the Duke of York	February 20,	1790
Richard Haworth	April 23,	1791
J. Braddyll	March 3,	1792
Thomas Scott	March 31,	1792

Sir John Hales	March 31,	1792
J. Nettleship	December 6,	1794
J. Mingay	March 21,	1795
Sir P. W. S. Gardiner	May 7,	1795
J. Walwyn	November 16,	1796
Thomas Potter	November 23,	1796
Dr. Thomas Mayo	January 21,	1798
R. Scudamore	January 27,	1798
James Green	February 3,	1798
Captain Wombwell	February 24,	1798
Edmond Estcourt	December 6,	1800
J. Trevanion, Jun.	March 7,	1801
Despard Croasdale	March 23,	1801
Sir Joseph Scott	March 23,	1805
John Kemble	May 4,	1805
J. Walsh	February 15,	1806
J. Nixon	March 15,	1806
Colonel Thomas Foley	February 7,	1807
John Richards	February 28,	1807
Sir J. Cox Hippersley, Bart.	March 5,	1808
Richard Wilson	March 26,	1808
H. R. H. the Duke of Sussex . .	April 30,	1808
Samuel James Arnold .	April 15,	1809
William Linley	February 17,	1810
Sir William Bolland (Baron of the Exchequer) .	April 7,	1810
H. N. Middleton	May 12,	1810
Lord Mountmorris	May 26,	1810
Colonel Wilson Braddyll .	March 9,	1812
W. J. Denison, M.P.	January 2,	1813
Henry Frederick Stephenson	May 8,	1813
Lord Grantley	November 20,	1814

Henry Brougham (Lord High Chancellor)	December 23,	1815
C. Marsh	March 16,	1816
Arthur Morris	March 23,	1816
Thomas Lewin	November 24,	1816
Robert Bill	November 24,	1816
Sir Mathew Wood, M.P.	March 15,	1817
Viscount Kirkwall	April 19,	1817
General Sir Ronald Fergusson, M.P.	February 14,	1818
Dr. Cooke	December 5,	1818
William Henry Whitbread, M.P.	March 6,	1819
James Lonsdale	March 27,	1819
Earl of Suffolk	April 22,	1820
Honourable Admiral G. Dundas	April 2,	1821
W. P. Honeywood	April 9,	1821
Colonel Thomas Wildman	December 8,	1821
Honourable A. Macdonald	February 2,	1822
Captain W. Terry	November 30,	1822
Robert Chaloner	May 3,	1823
The Duke of Leinster	June 7,	1823
Sir John Cam Hobhouse, M.P. (Lord Broughton)	May 13,	1824
Rowland Stephenson	May 29,	1824
Sir Francis Burdett, M.P.	June 11,	1825
Colonel W. Johnson	February 8,	1826
Knight of Kerry, M.P.	May 15,	1826
Charles William Hallett	April 27,	1827
Dr. Somerville	May 3,	1828
John Benjamin Heath (Baron Heath)	December 19,	1829
Lord Saltoun	November 27,	1830
General Sir Andrew Barnard	December 4,	1830
R. B. Peake	January 8,	1831
Honourable John Dundas, M.P.	March 19,	1831

Walter Campbell (of Islay), M.P.	June 11,	1831
Honourable Fox Maule, M.P. (Earl of Dalhousie)	January 9,	1836
Lord Methuen	March 12,	1836
Riversdale Grenfell, M.P.	April 23,	1836
Stewart Marjoribanks, M.P.	March 3,	1838
Archibald Hastie, M.P.	May 3,	1838
Augustus Walter Arnold	January 12,	1839
Dr. Thomas Mayo, Junr.	February 9,	1839
Dr. Somerville (re-elected)	May 3,	1839
Honourable Henry Howard, M.P.	May 25,	1839
Lord Frederick Gordon Hallyburton	May 25,	1839
Robert Liston	April 28,	1840
James Hope Vere	January 23,	1840
Colonel H. Webster	December 18,	1840
Captain Dalrymple, M.P. (Earl of Stair)	February 19,	1842
Robert Blagden Hale, M.P.	June 25,	1842
Colonel Robert Fergusson, M.P.	February 11,	1843
Mr. Serjeant Murphy, M.P.	May 18,	1844
Rowland Alston, M.P.	December 14,	1844
Dr. W. F. White	January 3,	1846
Honourable George O'Callaghan	January 3,	1846
Edward Lonsdale	February 5,	1848
Honourable Richard Howard	May 12,	1849
Augustus Keppel Stephenson	May 24,	1849
John Farley Leith	May 24,	1849
John Harcourt Powell	June 15,	1849
Honourable Frederick Ponsonby	November 16, 1850	
Thomas James Arnold	November 30, 1850	
Andrew Jardine	November 15, 1851	
J. R. Bulwer	November 4, 1854	
Edward Tredcroft	November 21, 1855	

Hon. Charles Wentworth Fitzwilliam, M.P. .	December 29,	1855
Henry Burnley Heath	February 9,	1856
Sir Charles Taylor (Sir Charles Taylor, Bart.) .	May 24,	1856
Honourable Alaster Fraser	February 21,	1857
Sussex Vane Stephenson	April 4,	1857
Sir Charles Locock, Bart.	May 30,	1857
Henry Robarts	March 20,	1858
Honourable Augustus Foley	April 2,	1859
G. B. Babington, M.D.	November 17,	1860
Colonel F. Marshall	November 17,	1860
John Jones	December 7,	1861
Earl of Strathmore	May 4,	1861
W. B. Gladstone	May 7,	1864
John Stirling Taylor	May 21,	1864
Junius Spencer Morgan	March 18,	1865
Robert Amadeus Heath	April 1,	1865
Russell Sturgis	February 23,	1866
The Earl of Dalhousie (re-elected) . . .	June 22,	1866

THE DINING-ROOM.   From a Sketch by James Hallett, Esq.

LIFE AND DEATH

OF THE

SUBLIME SOCIETY OF BEEF STEAKS.

T HERE is no doubt that a Beef-steak Club existed in London long before the formation of the Society which forms the subject of the present memoir.

Reference is made to such a Club in the "Spectator," * and in various contemporaneous works.

In later years other Beef-steak Clubs have sprung into existence, the most celebrated of which was one established in 1748, at the Dublin Theatre, presided over by Peg Woffington, the only female member. There was also a similar Club in Ivy Lane, London, among the members of which the name of Dr. Johnson appears. Cambridge had, and still has, its Beef-steak Club, and there were various others at Drury Lane Theatre, and elsewhere; but the fraternity which held together for 132 years, and has lately, to

* No. 9, March, 1710-11.

the regret of many, ceased to be, never from its earliest time called itself a Club, but was only recognised as THE SUBLIME SOCIETY OF BEEF STEAKS.

The Society was founded by Henry Rich, the celebrated harlequin and machinist of Covent Garden Theatre in 1735. Of him Garrick thus speaks in a prologue, when the innovation of a speaking pantomime first came into vogue,—

> " When Lun appeared, with matchless art and whim
> He gave the power of speech to every limb ;
> Tho' masked and mute conveyed his true intent,
> And told in frolic gestures what he meant ;
> But now the motley coat and sword of wood,
> Require a tongue to make them understood."

Rich was a man of rare wit and invention. In his room at Covent Garden (probably the painting-room), many of the eminent men of the time connected with literature, fashion, and the drama, used to assemble to have a chat with the witty machinist and his fellow labourer and friend George Lambert, described in the archives of the Society as "Landscape Painter."

There from time to time they partook, at two o'clock, of the hot steak dressed by Rich himself, accompanied by a "bottle of old port from the tavern hard by."

Thus the nucleus of a Brotherhood was formed which it is believed outlived in point of time any other convivial gathering.

The Sublime Society consisted of twenty-four members,

and the statement which has appeared in print that King George IV., when Prince of Wales, made an exception to the rule, is not borne out by the oldest traditions of the Society; on the contrary, it has been handed down from those who were contemporaneous members, that His Royal Highness, after having expressed a desire to belong to it, was obliged to wait his turn until a vacancy occurred.

In the earlier days of the Sublime Society of Beef Steaks, there appear, in addition to the names of Rich and Lambert, those of Churchill, Dennis Delane, Hogarth, Gabriel Hunt, Dean Price, Judge Welsh, Hippersley, Dr. Anthony Askew, (the donor of the Sword of State), John Beard, and Theophilus Cibber, &c., all well known men of their day. Then came, a little later, the Earl of Sandwich, George Coleman, Wilkes, John Beard (the singer), the Earls of Surrey and Effingham, John Kemble, the Prince of Wales, the Duke of York, and the Bard, Charles Morris.

Brother Morris was the life and soul of the Society. In it he lived, and may be said to have died. The author of "The Clubs of London," in speaking of the Bard's connection with the Beef Steaks, says,—

"Well has our laureate earned his wreath. At that table his best songs have been sung; for that table his best songs were written. His allegiance has been undivided. Neither hail, nor shower, nor snowstorm has kept him away; no engagement, no invitation, seduced him from it. I have seen him there 'out-watching the bear' in his 78th year ; for as yet nature had given no sign of decay in frame or faculty ; but you saw him in a green and vigorous old age, tripping mirthfully along the downhill of existence, without languor, or gout, or any of the penalties exacted by time for the mournful privilege of living. His face is still resplendent with cheerfulness.

"' Die when you will, Charles, you'll die in your youth.' Such were Curran's words, and they were amply verified."

Charles Morris died in 1838, at the age of 93, retaining unimpaired until within four days of his death the mental faculties of his youth.

* * * *

Saturday was from time immemorial the day of dining, and of late years the season commenced in November and ended in June.

Each member was allowed to bring one visitor. If he brought a second, he had to borrow a name ; in default of obtaining it, the visitor was doomed to retire.

In former times the members appeared in uniform, viz., a blue coat and buff waistcoat with brass buttons impressed with the gridiron and motto—" BEEF AND LIBERTY."

They also wore rings bearing the same devices.

* * * *

The Ring.

The Sublime Society of Beef Steaks has had during its existence strange vicissitudes. After the destruction of Covent
Garden Theatre, which for seventy years had been its home,
it migrated in 1808 to the Bedford Coffee-house, until the
building of the Old Lyceum in 1809.

There the Society remained until the burning of that Theatre
in 1830. After this, it adjourned to the Lyceum Tavern in
the Strand, and thence returned to the Bedford Coffee-house,
where it remained until 1838, when a suite of rooms was
built for it under the new roof of the Lyceum. The original
gridiron, dug out of the ruins of Covent Garden and the
Lyceum, formed the centre ornament of the dining-room ceiling. The entire room and ceiling were in Gothic architecture,
and the walls were hung with paintings and engravings of past
and present members, the former the work of Brother Lonsdale.
Folding-doors, the entire width of the room, connected it with
an anteroom. On the opening of these doors on the announce-
ment of dinner, an enormous grating in the form of a gridiron,
through which the fire was seen and the steaks handed, communicated with the kitchen. Over this gridiron were the lines:—

> " If it were done, when 'tis done, then 'twere well
> It were done quickly—"

Here the Sublime Society lived and died on beef-steaks.
Beef-steaks! such was the food—served hot and hot, and passed
from cook to serving-man through the gridiron referred to.

You heard them hissing—you saw the white-clad cook turning them with his tongs — the hot pewter plate was before you (changed on demand with every fresh steak). The accompaniments of baked potatoes, spanish onions cold and fried, beet root, and chopped eschalot were there, and at the close, when you wanted an extra excitement to induce you to eat one solitary mouthful more, you would aid in demolishing the last "shallotted steak," and join in the strife for possession of the final morsel that remained.

Toasted cheese ended the repast; and so appetising was the dinner, that with many who foreswore suppers, supper was the inevitable result. Porter (in pewter), port wine, punch and whisky toddy, were the accompaniments of this simple dinner. Smoking was permitted after THE SONG OF THE DAY, and THE USUAL TOAST.

The dinner ended, the cook in white cap and apron came round, pewter plate in hand, to collect the money.*

The first and last Saturdays of the season, and Saturday in Easter week were "Private."

On these days no visitors were invited. The accounts were gone into and the amount of the "whip," to regulate the past or accruing expenses, decided; the qualifications of such candidates as were anxious, on the occasion of a vacancy, to join

---

* Each member paid 5s. for his dinner, and 10s. 6d. for his guest. The entrance fee was £26 5s. to 1849, when it was reduced to £10 10s., and there were generally two annual whips of £5 each.

The President's Chair.

the Society, discussed ; and other matters connected with its
well-being, debated.

On the occurrence of an election, the formality of a ballot
was gone through, but a " No " was never dropped into the
bowl.

Every aspirant to that family circle was invited at least
twice as a guest that he might be impartially judged ; and he
was, *if put up*, certain of election.

The Society was thus constituted.

> THE PRESIDENT OF THE DAY.
> THE VICE-PRESIDENT.
> THE BISHOP.
> THE RECORDER.
> THE BOOTS.

The PRESIDENT took his seat after dinner throughout the
season according to the order in which his name appeared on
"the ROTA."

He was invested with the Badge of the Society by the
Boots. His duty was to give the chartered toasts in strict
accordance with the list before him ; to propose all resolutions
that had been duly made and seconded—to observe all the
ancient forms and customs of the Society, and to enforce them
on others. He had no sort of power inherent in his position ;—
on the contrary, he was closely watched and sharply pulled up
if he betrayed either ignorance or forgetfulness on the smallest

matter of routine connected with his office. In fact, he was a target for all to shoot at.

A Beef-eater's hat and plume hung on the right-hand side of the chair behind him, and a three-cornered hat (erroneously believed to have belonged to Garrick) on the left. When putting a resolution the President was bound to place the plumed hat on his head and instantly remove it. If he failed in one or the other act, he was speedily reminded by being called to order in no silent terms. The most important obligations imposed on him was the necessity of singing, whether he could sing or not, THE SONG OF THE DAY.

The VICE was the oldest member of the Society present, and had to carry out the President's directions without responsibility.

The BISHOP sang the Grace and the Anthem.

The RECORDER. The duty of the Recorder was very onerous. He had to rebuke everybody for offences, real or imaginary. His most important office was to deliver "the charge" to each newly elected member.

This was always a cause for great merriment; and such occasions, in which the highest joined, might be said to have more resembled a masquerade, or a set of schoolboys in their holidays, than the sober conduct of men of mature age. Those who have been parties to the Grand Court of Circuit, will more readily appreciate the hilarity of the proceeding.

On the initiation of a new member, he, and the visitors,

The Silver Badge.

were requested after dinner to withdraw to an ante-room, where port and punch were provided for them.

The newly elected member was then brought in blindfolded —accompanied on his right by the Bishop with his mitre on, and holding the volume in which the oath of allegiance to the rules of the Society was inscribed, while on his left stood some other member holding the sword of state. Behind were the halberdiers. These were all decked out in the most incongruous and absurd dresses—probably obtained originally from Covent Garden Theatre.

"The charge" was then delivered by the Recorder. In it he dwelt on the solemnity of the obligations the new member was about to take on himself. He was made to understand in tones alternately serious and gay, the true Brotherly spirit of the Sublime Society of Beef Steaks ; that while a perfect equality existed among the Brethren, such equality never should be permitted to degenerate into undue familiarity; that while badinage was encouraged in the freest sense of the word, such badinage must never approach to a personality ; and that good fellowship must be united with good breeding ; above all, attention was drawn to the Horatian motto over the chimney-piece ; and the aspirant was warned that ignominious expulsion was the fate of him who carried beyond those walls words uttered there in friendship's confidence.*

* Translation :—
    " Let none beyond this threshold bear away
    What friend to friend in confidence may say."

That done, the following oath, dating from the origin of the Society, was administered :—

OATH.

YOU SHALL ATTEND DULY,
VOTE IMPARTIALLY,
AND CONFORM TO OUR LAWS AND ORDERS OBEDIENTLY.
YOU SHALL SUPPORT OUR DIGNITY,
PROMOTE OUR WELFARE, AND AT ALL TIMES
BEHAVE AS A WORTHY MEMBER IN THIS SUBLIME SOCIETY.
SO BEEF AND LIBERTY BE YOUR REWARD.

This was read aloud clause by clause by the Bishop, and repeated by the candidate; at the end, the book was rapidly exchanged by the Serjeant * for the bone of beef that had served for the day's dinner, carefully protected by a napkin, and after the words,

"SO BEEF AND LIBERTY BE MY REWARD,"

he was desired to kiss the book. Instead of this he kissed its substitute; and by reason of a friendly downward pressure from behind, he generally did so most devoutly.

The bandage was then removed from his eyes; the book on which he had sworn the oath was still before him; and amid the laughter and congratulations of his Brethren, he again

* The cook.

10

The Sword.

took his seat as a Member of the Sublime Society, and the excluded guests were re-admitted.

The "Boots" was the last elected of the members; and there was a grave responsibility attached to his office. He was the fag of the brotherhood, and sometimes a hard life he had of it.

It was his duty to arrive before the dinner-hour; not only to decant the wine, but to fetch it from the cellar. This latter custom was persevered in until the destruction of the old Lyceum by fire, and was only then abandoned by reason of the inaccessibility of the cellar when the Society returned to the new Theatre, the present Lyceum, in 1838. No one was exempted from this ordeal; and woe to him who shirked or neglected it. The greatest enjoyment seemed to be afforded, both to members and guests, by summoning "Boots" to decant a fresh bottle of port at the moment when a hot plate and a fresh steak were placed before him.

The Duke of Sussex was Boots from the date of his election (April, 1808), to April, 1809, when a vacancy occurred and my father was elected, releasing His Royal Highness from the post. Indeed, until the Society ceased to exist, the Duke of Leinster, who had duly served his apprenticeship, (although he drank nothing stronger than water himself) constantly usurped the legitimate duties of the "Boots," by arriving before him, and performing the accustomed, but not forgotten, services of the day.

When any "Boots" showed signs of temper, or any member was unruly, or infringed the rules of the Society, a punishment was in store for him. It was moved and seconded that such delinquent should be put in the white sheet, and reprimanded by the Recorder; and if the "Ayes had it," (and they always did have it) the sentence was carried out.

The offending party was taken from the room by two members bearing halberts, and preceded by a third carrying the sword, and was brought back again in the garb of penitence (the table-cloth). Then, after a lecture from the Recorder, severe or humorous according to the nature of his offence, he was allowed to resume his place at the table.

It happened that Brother the Duke of Sussex was put in the white sheet, under the following circumstances. His Royal Highness had come to the Steaks with Brother Hallett, and on the road the watch-chain belonging to the latter had been cut, and his bunch of seals stolen. The cloth removed, Hallett addressed the President, recounted the loss he had sustained, and charged the Duke as the perpetrator of the robbery. The case was tried on the spot, and the evidence having clearly established the criminality of the accused (to a Beef-Steak Jury) it was moved and resolved that H.R.H. should forthwith be put into the white sheet and reprimanded for an act which might have been considered a fault had the victim been a stranger, but which became a crime when that victim was a Brother. There was no appeal. His Royal Highness reluctantly rose—was taken out in custody—brought before the Recorder (Brother Richards), and received a witty, but unsparing admonition for the offence, of which he had been unanimously found guilty. For a wonder, His Róyal Highness took it ill. He resumed his seat; but remained silent and reserved. No wit could make him smile—no bantering could rouse him—and at an unusually early hour he ordered his carriage and went away.

The next day my father, who had been the mover of the resolution, went to the Palace to smooth the ruffled plumes of his Royal *confrère*, and took me with him. In those days the Duke rode on horseback, and as we turned out of the gate leading from the gardens to the portico, his horse was at the door, and His Royal Highness in the act of coming out. By the time we neared the entrance his foot was in the stirrup, and he saw us approaching. Without a moment's hesitation he withdrew his foot, released the bridle, and with both his enormous hands extended, advanced three or four steps to meet my father.

"I know what you're come about," he called loudly out in his accustomed note (probably B flat) and wringing both my father's hands until he winced with pain; "I know what you've come about! I made a fool of myself last night. You were quite right and I quite wrong—so I shall come next Saturday and do penance again for my bad temper!"

Such was the gracious reception of His Royal Highness;

and this said and done while the sentries were presenting arms, and his Highlander and grooms standing by the horses.

*   *   *   *

As I myself was the last culprit who underwent the punishment of the white sheet before the dissolution of the Society, it may not be considered egotistical if I here allude to it.

It was on the 15th of January, 1866, an occasion which will be long remembered by the Steakers, when the Society was honoured by the presence of many distinguished guests.

I chanced to be the President of the day. The cloth removed, it became my duty to propose, as the fourth toast, "Our worthy visitors," a ceremony which involved the necessity of naming each one in succession.

Brother Dalhousie dined on that day as an honorary member, and his name was included by me in the list of visitors—fearing, if I omitted it, that which I was sure to receive either way—a reprimand.

The healths drunk, I was doomed to pay the anticipated penalty.

It was moved, seconded, and carried unanimously, "That the President be put into a white sheet and rebuked for his want of courtesy to a Brother, and for his utter ignorance of the Rules of the Society."

A general rise took place—the sword was seized by the

slighted member—two others, who delighted in my disgrace, rushed to the halberts. I was forthwith compelled to leave the chair; my badge of office was removed, and I was hurried from the room. When re-conducted I was made to stand, clothed in white, between an illustrious guest and Brother the Duke of Leinster (my former Vice but who now occupied my seat as President), and received from him the reprimand he administered, with, I hope, becoming contrition for my fault. That done, the badge was replaced, and I was allowed to resume my seat and fulfil, as best I could, my remaining duties: the last act of my reign having been to move that Brother Dalhousie should be re-admitted, at his own request, a member of the Sublime Society.

*   *   *   *

Singing was always from its earliest days, a leading feature in the Society, both as regarded its members and their visitors, who were always invited to "assume a virtue if they had it not."

Who, having often dined at the Steaks, will forget our Treasurer's daily invitation, "If you wish to hear me sing, come listen to my ditty;" or Brother Saltoun's "On the 24th of October, when at Spithead we lay;" or Brother Brougham's unique song, "La pipe de tabac;" or Brother Dalhousie's familiar "Come ye from Athol, lad?" or Brother Hastie's "Muirland Meg;" or the witty songs of our Irish Brethren,

George O'Callaghan, Frederick Ponsonby, and Johnny Jones; or the rich toned voices of Brothers Dundas and Tredcroft, or the songs so full of sentiment of Brothers Stair and Locock? Or, above all, who, having heard them, will forget the inimitable songs written and sung by Brother Hallett, and here, I believe, for the first time, published?

*   *   *   *

The friendly equality that existed among the members of the Sublime Society of Beef Steaks, tempered always by good breeding, constituted one of its principal charms.

Give and take was the order of the day—the smartest things were uttered—the happiest retorts responded—yet all was said and done in a truly Beefsteak spirit. Offence was never meant, and rarely taken. If any member had a weak point, his faulty armour was speedily pierced. That small school-room had only twenty-four scholars; but as in the larger public ones, each pupil found his level there. If a man showed signs of wincing under the lash of a sarcasm, or was nettled by a bantering he could not perhaps reply to, he became at once a butt. If his temper could not brook the playful ordeal, the Society was not his home, and he and it parted.

I remember one esteemed member who turned sulky. He was put into the white sheet and brought before the President who admonished him as a parent would a child,—a Beefsteak sermon without its usual bathos. The recipient listened to the harangue without moving a muscle of his face. The lecture done, he resumed his seat, and at the next meeting sent in his resignation.

The love of "chaffing," which entered so largely into the elements of good fellowship with the Sublime Society was never, under any circumstances, permitted with the visitors. They were treated with the utmost distinction. They were never unduly urged to drink more than might be agreeable to them; one bumper in the evening was alone imperative; but it might be drunk in water. They were never pressed, though always asked to sing. A "suggestion" to sing was the adopted word.

Many of our visitors have added largely to the evening's amusements by their wit and vocal powers.

Amongst others the songs of Michael Blood, The Hon. Frederick Cadogan, James Hallett, Samuel Lover, Dr. Lavies, and "The Little Bil-ly" of Thackeray, will not be forgotten either by guests or members. To the former we were always indebted for their ready kindness and sociability.

From time immemorial it had been the custom for the President to propose the visitors' healths separately. That done—and as all speeches were prohibited—they were expected to rise simultaneously to return thanks as best they might.

It was a great source of amusement to see the doubt and

anxiety of the uninitiated as to who should take precedence in acknowledging the toast. On such occasions the bold who sought to do so were vociferously applauded until they found their reiterated efforts an impossibility; the nervous were encouraged only to meet with a similar fate. At length, when a pause in the enthusiasm gave some would-be speaker the hope of uttering a graceful compliment, the "Bravos" of the members became so general that the visitors resumed their seats. It was then proposed, seconded, and carried, "that the speeches of the worthy visitors be taken down separately and printed at the expense of the Society."

The only call to which it was imperative for a visitor to respond was "a toast." If he hesitated too long he was, perhaps abruptly, told he might give anything the world produced; man, woman or child, or any sentiment, social or otherwise. Sometimes it happened that such prompting was in vain, and the confused guest would nine times out of ten propose the only toast he was prohibited from giving, "The prosperity of the Sublime Society of Beef Steaks."

Although all badinage was prohibited as regarded guests, practical jokes were sometimes indulged in.

On one occasion, when a large and distinguished party had met, a wealthy and somewhat pretentious Liverpool merchant was invited as a guest by Brother Lonsdale. From something that occurred this gentleman conceived the idea that the royal and titled persons to whom he had been presented were myths, and he communicated this conviction to his host, adding that the joke was a good one, but that he had seen through it. The humour of the idea was instantly seized, and in a few seconds the Sublime Society was by tacit consent transformed into a Society of Traders. The Duke of Sussex reproached Alderman Wood for the tough steaks he had sent last Saturday,—Wood retorted on his Royal Brother by protesting against the misfitting stays he had sent his wife. Brother Burdett told Whitbread his last cask of beer was sour, who accounted for it by its having been kept too long in the Tower, &c., &c.

The suspicions of the guest were now confirmed, and warmed by the belief that his penetration had broken up the hoax as to a rank the members no longer cared to assume, sarcastically addressed those to whom he had been specially introduced by their real titles. His conviction was strengthened by what occurred after dinner. To shorten the table, a leaf had to be withdrawn. In closing it, the President's chair, occupied by Brother the Duke of Leinster, was overbalanced, and both Duke and chair fell backwards into the grate. No one moved, a roar of laughter succeeded the fall, in the midst of which the Duke scrambled up as best he could, replaced his chair, and resumed his seat.

In relating afterwards this anecdote, the sceptical guest quoted the above incident as a conclusive proof that his friend had tried to take him in as to the quality of the persons he had been invited to meet,—"Why," he said, "they wanted me to believe the chairman was the Duke of Leinster! as if when he fell into the grate, had he been a real Duke, they would not all have helped to pick him up!"

One among many of the distinguished literary men who were guests of the Society, was Hogg, the Ettrick Shepherd, who gave the following account of his visit in "The Shepherd's Noctes," published in Fraser's Magazine in July, 1833.

Gilfillan.—"O man! there is nothing I like sae weel as your stories about London. We saw by the papers that you were in a great number of public societies as a guest. Which of them all did you enjoy most?"

Shepherd.—"O! The Beef-Steak Club out o' a' sight!"

Simon.—"The Beef-Steak Club?—a curious denomination! What sort of a society is that?"

Shepherd.—"Ah, Sim! the queerest set o' devils that ever were conjoined thegither. A' noblemen an' first-rate gentlemen, though, for a' their michievous tricks. I never was with the hempies but ae night, by particular invitation, alang wi' Murray; but I never leugh as muckle on a night sin' I was born. O, I wad like to be a member o' the Beef-Steak Club! But that's impossible, as they are a' far aboon my sphere, an' I live ower far frae them. An' mair than that, by a clause in their original institution, the number is limited, which is a great pity. The late king, when Prince of Wales, had to wait three years after he applied, before he could be admitted; and only got in by sending a nobleman abroad to a lucrative situation! When Mr. Murray and I went in, the first service of Beef-steaks was just serving, and the Recorder was on his legs reading some apologies. The first was from the Duke of Leinster, whose turn it was to have filled the chair that night, but who found it out of his power to reach London in time. There was one from the Lord Chancellor, who was detained by the illness of a darling daughter; and one from the Duke of Wellington, on account of precarious health."

Gilfillan.—"And what is it about the Club that delighted you so much? Do they actually dine on Beef-steaks?"

Shepherd.—"Solely on Beef-steaks—but what glorious Beef-steaks! They do not come up all at once, as we get them in Scotland—no, nor half-a-dozen times; but up they come at long intervals, thick, tender, and as hot as fire. And during these intervals they sit drinking their port, and breaking their wicked wit on each other, so that every time a service of new steaks came up, we fell to them with much the same zest as at the beginning. The dinner, I think, would last from two to three hours, and was a perfect treat—a feast without alloy."

Simon.—"What! do they drink port during dinner?"

Shepherd.—"They do that, Billy. If ony member had ca'd for aught aboon port, I wadna hae been i' his line for forty shillings, as the bogle said. In the first place, he wad hae been fined; in the second, he wad hae been obliged to take a public rebuke. Ony o' them may hae as muckle punch as they like, or toddy, or twist; but wine of a nominal higher quality than port they are not allowed to taste. The Hon. Lord Saltoun, who was unanimously voted into the chair, had committed a high and serious offence to the Club that night; so he was adjudged to stand with a white sheet about him, while the Recorder-general put on his cocked hat, and gave him a very sharp and cutting rebuke, but in a style of ludicrous sublimity quite indescribable. What do you think was Saltoun's offence? I'll defy ony living man to guess. It was for sending a dozen bottles of sublime Highland whisky from his own stock, for the use of the Society, without leave granted. It is a club in which nae man can ken whether he is doing right or wrong; the kindest action may be accounted an offence; but always the more *outré* a man's behaviour is the better. The greatest offence of all is to lose temper. No man is there allowed to lose his temper on pain of being turned out of the Society. It is no uncommon thing for a gentleman to be fined and rebuked for his face growing red. The Club seems to have been originally formed to teach men good temper, good humour and forbearance; and certainly there never was a better school established, for there is no sly insinuation that can be brought forward against each other that is neglected, and always brought forward in the most laughable and extravagant terms. During the whole evening the conversation was so constant and so hearty, that, save when a gentleman got up, who was always listened to, no man could hear a word of the conversation, save from his next neighbours."

Gilfillan.—" How were you placed?"

Shepherd.—" I was near the head of the table, with Sir John Hobhouse above me on my left, and the Recorder on my right."

Gilfillan.—" O, man! how I would have liked to have been in your place!"

Shepherd.—" Are you a Whig?"

Gilfillan.—" No, no—you have nothing ado with that. But tell us what sort of a gentleman Sir John is."

Shepherd.—" A thin chap, wi' a Wellington face—rather younger looking than I expected; and appeared, that night at least, modest and unassuming in his manners. As for the Recorder, his tongue never lay for a moment; but then his good humour was inexhaustible. The croupier, a real clever chield, with ane o' the glibbest

tongues that ever waggit within teeth, got up and gave his honour
the Recorder a severe reprimand for havering sae muckle to me,
whereby no one could get a word exchanged with me but himself.
But he just hotched, an' leugh, an' gaed on. He told me a great
number of anecdotes regarding the Club, which I was sorry I could
not with any propriety take notes of, for they were very queer
indeed. There was one which struck me as particularly whimsical.
Lord Brougham, said to be the greatest wag among them, adjudged
an honourable member one night, for some alleged misdemeanour,
to walk three times round the company with a white sheet about
him. The culprit obeyed without the least hesitation, and
swaggered majestically round the apartment so equipt. I shall
give you only one trait more of this singular society. Campbell of
Islay sat over against me, next to the president but one, and
observing that his chair was generally empty, I asked the Recorder
the reason of it, who told me that Islay was Boots to the ·Club,
being the youngest member. He had everything to do as far as
drinkables were concerned—to draw all the wine, decant, and
arrange it. The landlord and waiter, when present, were not
suffered to do anything, save to break their jokes on the members ;
so that really on such a night, when the Club was so numerous, the
member for Argyle's berth was no sinecure. They dine on Saturdays at the Bedford Coffee-house, somewhere, I think about the
laigirs o' Covent Garden, and always part before twelve. O, it is a
joyous Club !"

*   *   *   *

Members were responsible for their guests, who were made to understand that whatever passed within the walls of the S. S. B. S. was sacred. William Jerdan, Editor of the " Literary Gazette," was a visitor, and at a late hour he was observed to take a note of a brilliant repartee that had been made.

The President, by whose side he sat, pointed to the motto over the chimney-piece—

" Ne fidos inter amicos
Sit, qui dicta foras eliminet."

" Jerdan," he said, " you understand those words ? "

" I understand one," said Jerdan, looking sharply round, "*sit*, and I mean to do it."

*　　　*　　　*　　　*

" Why did such a society collapse " is a question often asked, and one not easily answered.

In so limited a circle, attractive as it always had been by reason of the combination it presented of talent, wit, and good fellowship, it is needless to say that the presence of Royalty enhanced its celebrity, or that the absence of so distinguished an element affected its prosperity.

To be elected a member of that Brotherly band was, at one

time, a distinction coveted by many but of necessity conferred on few ; and although other Royal personages have since from time to time been its honoured guests, still, with the retirement of His Royal Highness the Duke of Sussex in 1839 (the third member of the Royal House), the traditionary pride of having a prince of the blood associated with the Sublime Society of Beef Steaks became a thing of the past. Notwithstanding this, it maintained its reputation. It continued to count in its ranks Cabinet Ministers, politicians—men eminent in most of the liberal professions and in commerce—and men who were noted for their wit and other social qualities ; amongst all of whom a perfect cordiality existed, based on the intimate acquaintance of many years ; and the friendly epithet of "Brother" adopted by the members in their social intercourse was not an empty word.

Friendships were there formed which may be truly said to have outlived the Society, and to the perfect freedom and equality which existed at that board, those who are living can testify.

Still, for very many years past, symptoms of its decadence became manifest, and the class of men who might have been willing to enter into the spirit of the Society, and who could have added to its conviviality and enlivened it by their wit, were difficult to find. The retirement of Brother Brougham was a severe blow to the Society. He had been so constant an attendant—his brilliant repartees and flow of spirits had been so thoroughly congenial, that his loss it is impossible to overestimate.

Four years before he was made Chancellor the following resolution appears in the book of the Society.

"In May, 1826, it was resolved that a pipe of port wine should be presented, by permission, to this Society, by Brother Brougham or Brother Stephenson : by him who should be first appointed to the office of Lord Chancellor of Great Britain—first singer at the French Opera—Master of the Rolls, or Master in Chancery."

This note was followed by a later one.

"Brother Brougham was promoted to the office of Lord Chancellor on the 28th November, 1830, and therefore was permitted to present a pipe of port to the Society."*

This is succeeded by the following note.

"1831, January 15th.

"The calamitous fire which destroyed the English Opera-House in February, 1830, having, among its many disastrous consequences, destroyed also that refuge and domicilium of the Sublime Society of Beef Steaks, which it had found after a similar misfortune that occasioned the destruction of Covent Garden Theatre,

---

* No presents were allowed to be made to the Sublime Society, unless permission to offer them had been previously granted.

(whence, where it had been originally founded and where it had flourished for more than seventy years, the Sublime Society of Beef Steaks was, on the rebuilding of that Theatre, cruelly and unjustly excluded), the Society being thus without a shelter, was compelled to seek a temporary refuge in a house of public entertainment. While suffering under this distress and with the hope of a speedy restoration of the English Opera-House, it pleased his Majesty, William IV., to select one of its distinguished members, and appoint him to the office and dignity of Lord High Chancellor of Great Britain. The Society not deeming it to be consistent with the station of their Brother that he should there visit them at a meeting of the board held at such a place, adjourned to his house in Berkeley Square, he earnestly desiring to be present with his Brethren in proof of his steady attachment to the Society. The meeting was accordingly held at the house of the Lord Chancellor, the day being a private day."

Brother Brougham, after his retirement in 1835, only dined with the Society twice; on the 23rd June, and the 28th November, 1838.

His secession was followed a few years later by that of the Duke of Sussex, and by the deaths of many of the old members.

The resignation of Brother Broughton, in 1856, after having been for thirty-three years a member, may in late years be considered as the beginning of the end. That he himself shared in the regrets he caused the Society at large by his cessation, is shown by the following correspondence.

"ERLE STOKE, WESTBURY,
"29 *October*, 1856.

"MY DEAR STEPHENSON,

"'There is a time for all things,' the wise man has said ; and I feel that the day has come when I must retire from the society in which I have passed so many happy hours. If I have ever added anything to the gaiety and good fellowship of the Brotherhood, I am aware that I can contribute nothing to them now, and I am unwilling to linger amongst those, to whom it would be more becoming in me and agreeable to them that I should bid an affectionate farewell. Be so good as to communicate this intention of mine to our friends of the S. S. B. S., and assure them of my sincere wishes for the 'prosperity and long continuance of their Society.'
"Believe me, My dear Stephenson,
"To be very truly yours,
"BROUGHTON."

"6, ST. GEORGE'S PLACE, HYDE PARK CORNER,
"*October* 30, 1856.

"MY DEAR BROUGHTON,

"I have received your letter of resignation as a Brother of the S. S. B. S. with regret, but not with surprise. I have long observed the lingering wish to go, and you have taken courage to depart, like the Roman in the Capitol, that you may adjust your mantle ere you fall. I had hoped that, as you and I had so long journeyed together, we should have travelled on till the final departure of the one of us. As to myself, I have still somewhat of the gamesome spirit of the old Roman Antony—although the grey doth mingle with my brown—and shall consider the good old Steaks as my Cleopatra whose 'custom cannot stale her infinite variety,' and who still makes hungry where most she satisfies. You have, according to the light of your understanding, done what you think to be right. I shall blunder yet a little longer in my twilight, and shall always remember with affectionate pleasure the many canty days we have had with one another in our fraternal intercourse. I know not whether it will be agreeable to you that you should still remain as an honorary member, if so, you must be assured of the pleasure it will give to us all to see you again at the Board.

" Believe me, My dear Broughton,

" To be sincerely yours,

" HENRY FREDERICK STEPHENSON."

" ERLE STOKE, WESTBURY,

" 31 October, 1856.

MY DEAR STEPHENSON,

" Many thanks for your kind letter and for your gratifying proposal. I think, however, that, in matters of this sort, what is done should be completely done, and I am sure that if I was elected an honorary member of the S. S. B. S., and ever came amongst you, I should repent of my retirement. It was ' multum gemens ' that I brought myself to send you my resignation. As for your leaving the Society, I am convinced, as I ventured to tell our friends one day when you were absent, that your loss would be fatal to the concern. It would not and will not survive you, and when I wished prosperity and long continuance to it, I only used the words of our concluding toast, as involving the same benefit to you. Again, farewell as a colleague, not, I trust, to separate from you as a friend.

" Ever sincerely yours,

" BROUGHTON."

Brother Broughton never dined again with the Society.

It was hoped, on the occasion I have before referred to (the 15th January, 1866) that his health would permit him once more to join his old friends beneath the gridiron. But this was not to be. As a visitor, he was invited. I record the sad answer I received.

"Ah, my dear Arnold, you are too kind ; and would charm the bird off the bough. But, alas ! and alas ! I am totally unfit for such treats as those with which you tempt me.

"I have not dined anywhere for many a long month, and the next repast at which I shall, in all probability, assist, will be, like that of Polonius—not where I eat, but am eaten.

"Ever truly yours,

"BROUGHTON."

*   *   *   *

But the crowning disaster that befel the Sublime Society was the death of its Treasurer and Secretary, Henry Frederick Stephenson, in 1858.

With him in truth it died. Elected a member in 1813, he was the connecting link between a past and present generation ; with his career as " man and boy," to use his own expression (he said he grew younger every year)—were associated in intimate relationship many well known men of the day. With him flourished as Beef Steak Brothers—all but two of a past generation—

The Duke of Norfolk (who introduced him).
Charles Morris (the Bard).
John Kemble.
John Richards, the Recorder.
Richard Wilson.
H.R.H. The Duke of Sussex.
Samuel James Arnold.
Lord Mountnorris.
William Linley.
Sir William Bolland.
Lord Grantley.
Henry Brougham, M.P. (Lord Brougham).
Sir Matthew Wood, M. P.
W. J. Denison, M.P.
Sir Ronald Fergusson, M.P.
W. H. Whitbread, M.P.
James Lonsdale.
The Earl of Suffolk.
Admiral Dundas.
*The Duke of Leinster.
The Right Hon. Sir John Cam Hobhouse (Lord Broughton).
Sir Francis Burdett, M.P.
The Knight of Kerry, M.P.
C. W. Hallett.
*The Right Hon. Fox Maule (The Earl of Dalhousie).

The spirit of the day in which those men lived, never to the last deserted Brother Stephenson : his inborn geniality, fostered by such associates, clung to him to his dying day.

The blue coat with brass buttons, the buff waistcoat, the tights and hessians, the alternate grave and brightened face,

* The sole survivors.

the cheery laugh, the unflagging spirits, contagious in their mirth, the sharp attack or rapid repartee, all so familiar to many who will read these lines, were the type of a passing but not then extinct phase of society.

He was the Shepherd of the flock ; while he lived, he kept them in the fold ; when he died, they strayed.

> " The evil that men do lives after them,
> The good is oft interred with their bones."

It has been often urged that the freedom of speech he indulged in, sparing neither friend nor foe, excluded many from the Society. It may be so ; but certain it is that the non-contents were far outnumbered by those who were only too glad to be enlivened by the good fellowship which was inherent in himself, and which he engendered in others.

None who knew Brother Stephenson will call to mind his convivial qualities, and his open and generous nature, without the conviction that his loss was irreparable.

The verse added to the obituary anthem by Brother Ponsonby speaks in few words the feeling of the survivors.

> " Our Stephenson's gone, whose bright fancy gave birth
> To shrewd maxims of wit set in flashes of mirth,
> The last of the giants that lingered on earth,
> 'Mid the jolly old Steakers of England."

No wonder that when he died the prediction of Brother Broughton, written in 1856, should in 1867 be verified.*

* See ante, p. 29.

"Your loss," he wrote, "would be fatal to the concern. It would not and will not survive you."

*   *   *   *

In the meantime, gradual changes crept over the Society; imperceptible at first, but with each succeeding year more and more pronounced.

The declining, did not amalgamate with the rising generation. All the time-honoured observances—follies though they were— that had been part of a system with the Sublime Society of Beef Steaks, were gradually sought to be ignored by modern members. Society, in its progression, was antagonistic to the old and venerated customs which for a century and a quarter had known no change. The blue coat and buff waistcoat were discarded; the ring, if occasionally produced, was a curiosity to be handed round as an object of art of the olden time.

"Boots," whose duties have been already explained, would come too late to decant the Port, and was sometimes known to be guilty of the crime of persisting in finishing his hot steak when called on for a fresh bottle. Indeed, the revolutionary principle had been carried so far, that he had of late been known to let the Serjeant do the duty for him.

The contagion of insubordination extended even to our respected visitors.

The old custom of their rising simultaneously to return

thanks on the occasion of their healths being drunk, began to be disregarded. They became occasionally recalcitrant. They sometimes would not and did not rise; the humour of the thing, such as it was, ceased to be in vogue, and thus another habit of the olden time languished, if it did not actually die.

Another modern objection that arose from the changes which affected society at large, was our day of dining. Saturday was, during the season, a dinner-giving day—and often deprived us both of members and visitors. The railways were antagonistic to our interests, and carried away many to their country homes. On the evening of that day Lady Palmerston received; and the result of all this was a constant drain on our resources.

In 1865 the experiment was tried of changing the day of meeting from Saturday to Friday; but the result was not a happy one, and the once crowded room remained comparatively forsaken.

Gout, too, had asserted its supremacy, and port wine drinking was tabooed. A compromise was effected, and another innovation allowed—sherry was introduced.

The proverbial tenderness of our steaks now began to be assailed.

He, who had for years with true artistic skill preserved and furnished us on each succeeding Saturday with three rumps of beef;—who, were the party unusually large and, as it sometimes happened, the demand exceeded the supply, would rush out to satisfy the call for "More steaks!" or would, without a murmur, take back what remained were the party small;—he

> " Who would blush when we praised him,
> Or weep when we blamed;"

who had humoured our many whims and consulted our varied tastes and appetites without a word;—who had responded so long to the energetic calls from many voices for "A hot steak!" "A thick steak!" "A thin steak!" "An underdone steak!" "A steak not done so much!" "A shallotted steak!" "A plain steak!"—even he, when the ideal consumption of three rumps became a mockery, and of only one almost a satire,—he, who had served us for many years in our prosperity, abandoned us in our decline.

The Butcher sent in his resignation.*

Next, our time of dining was objectionable. By gradations it had advanced from two to seven. In 1808 the hour was four. In 1833 it was changed from five to six, and in 1861 from six to seven. But seven was too early for the afternoon park, so in 1866 the last change was made, and we dined at eight.

The result was that while on the one hand many of the old members who were wont to finish the night at "The little Theatre in the Haymarket," or at Drury Lane, or Covent Garden, the Lyceum or Adelphi (they would have had a

---

* The beef was sent with a man to cut it; what was not eaten was taken back. The average price the Society paid was 2s. 6d. a lb.

greater choice now-a-days), were debarred from their accustomed lounge; the innovation on the other hand was productive of no permanent good.

Modern refinement objected to our very toasts! and even they, for a while, were re-modelled.

But the time had passed when any such changes could stem the tide of events. The inevitable was at hand.

After the death of Brother Stephenson, the Society suffered from a sensible diminution of its old members, many of whom it could not replace. It lost the two sons of the Treasurer, Brothers Augustus and Sussex Stephenson, Baron Heath, J. F. Leith, the Earl of Dalhousie and Tom Arnold (irreverently called Brother Beak, but who returned to his allegiance in 1865; as did Brother Dalhousie in the following year), Colonel Marshall, Dr. Babington, The Honourable A. Fraser, and J. R. Bulwer.

New members—acquisitions in every sense to any society—entered the ranks, but the discipline was gone. The elements of intimacy and sociability so patent in the past were wanting in the present. It was not the dinner, good as it at most times was, that brought that brotherly band together. There existed among them all, a bond of union, a spirit of freemasonry without its mysteries, which made them cling together. But all this died out as old friends passed away. In later days notes were exchanged between intimates to know if they should meet, and it became a habit to enquire before entering the rooms as to who, if any one, had arrived.

Many a man has turned back to dine at his club with a feeling of disappointment in his heart and a sigh for the good old times, when he has found that no one was there, or that only comparative strangers occupied the places of old and valued friends.

From the same cause the attendance of visitors became restricted. Members grew diffident as to inviting guests, fearing lest in lieu of the brilliant evening they had been led from tradition to expect, they might find "a beggarly account of empty" chairs,—or an effort at gaiety, usurping the place of wit and song.

The books wherein the names of host and guest are recorded for very many years show strange vicissitudes of late. Seven times in the season of 1866-7 the President's chair was vacant, and the room empty; and seven other times a solitary signature adorned the page. Probably the dinners of these self-sacrificing members were not over gay. On such occasions the room became sepulchral; the table, always laid for ten or twelve, looked ghastly; the hot steaks came and went in too rapid succession, while the waiters dimly glided to and fro. At last when the solitary one was shut in and left alone with his bottle of old port and his bowl of punch or whisky toddy (if he had had the heart to make it), and, reckless of his duty, the list of unuttered toasts lay beside him, it is not unlikely that he looked at the portraits surrounding him in that silent room of the living and the dead, until the memories of the past made them once more his companions and his friends.

*   *   *   *

When the struggle ended, in 1867, the rota stood thus :—

	ELECTED.	RE-ELECTED.
W. H. Whitbread	1819	
The Duke of Leinster	1823	
The Earl of Dalhousie	1836	1866
Walter Arnold	1839	
The Earl of Stair	1842	
Robert B. Hale	1842	
Hon. Frederick Ponsonby	1850	
Tom Arnold	1850	1865
A. Jardine	1851	
Hon. Charles Fitzwilliam, M.P.	1855	
Henry B. Heath	1856	
Sir Charles Locock, Bart.	1857	
Henry Robarts	1858	
Hon. Colonel Foley	1859	
W. R. Gladstone	1864	
J. Stirling Taylor	1864	
F. S. Morgan	1865	
Russell Sturgis	1866	

Of this list of eighteen members, Brother Whitbread was, at the time of his death, the oldest. I never knew him to dine but once with the Society during the twenty-eight years I belonged to it. Of the remaining seventeen, nine resided in the country, and in the last season their united attendances amounted to ten.

During the twenty-nine days we dined together (?), fifty-nine members attended, making an average of two a day! Need more be said ?

＊   ＊   ＊   ＊

Here closes my slight memoir.

The writing it has caused me pleasure and pain.

If I have dwelt at too great length on seeming trifles, the fault is due to my attachment for the old customs of a Society with which I have hereditary and personal associations during nearly half its long existence.

I there received so much sympathy and kindness that I cling to its memory.   I entered it with pride ; I have lost it with regret.

WALTER   ARNOLD.

THE ALBANY, *December*, 1870.

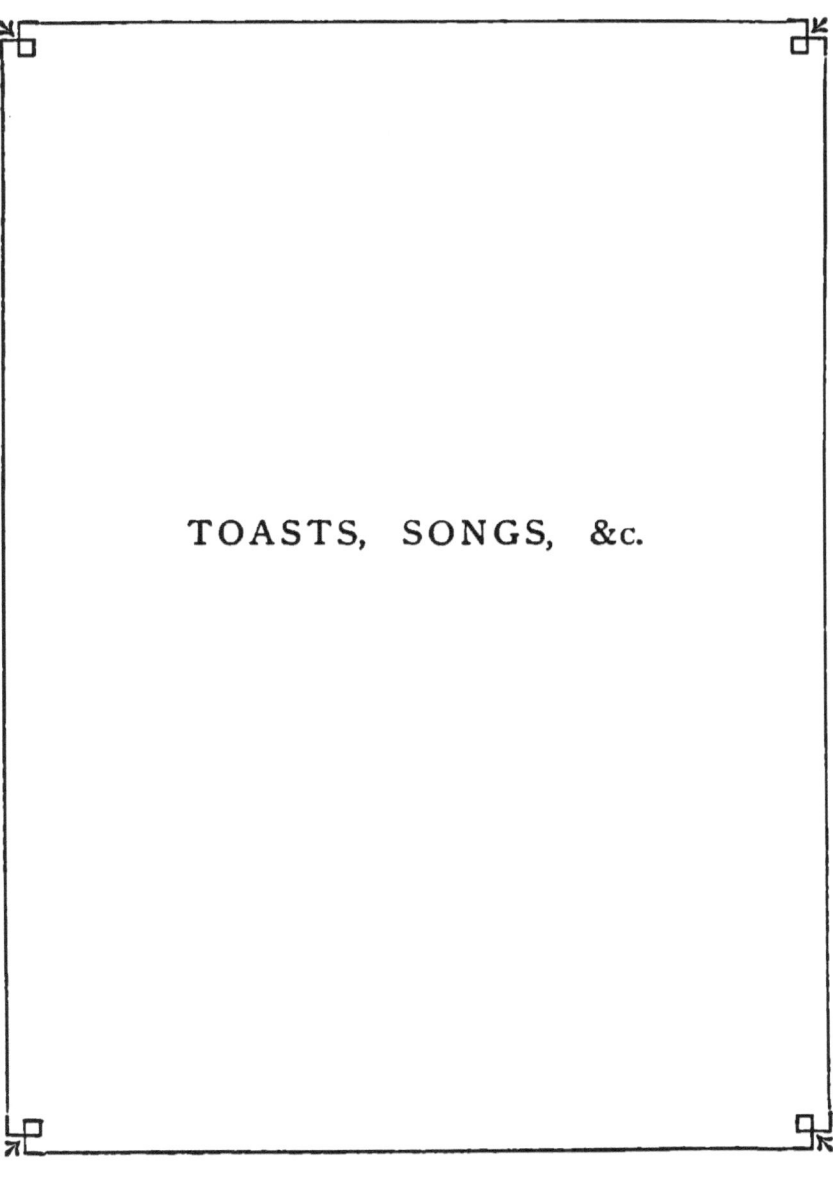

TOASTS, SONGS, &c.

TOASTS, SONGS,

&c.

GRACE. Sung by the Bishop.

Her Majesty and the Royal Family.

The President's Health.

The President Elect.

Our Worthy Visitors.

The Song of the Day and the Usual Toast.

The Visitor's Toasts.

The Members' Toasts, beginning with the President.

To our deceased Friends, who have been Members of this
Society.

Success to Mr. Arnold, and prosperity to this Theatre.*

To the Memory of Mr. Rich, and long Continuance to this
Society.

* This toast was added after the opening of the old Lyceum Theatre, in 1809.

The Song of the Day.

Written by Brother THEODOSIUS FORREST.

No more shall Fame ex-pand her wings To sound of He-roes,

States, or Kings; A no - bler flight the God - dess takes, To

praise our Brit- ish Beef in Steaks; A joy - ful theme for

(CHORUS.)

Bri-tons free, Hap-py in Beef and Li - ber- ty. A

joy-ful theme for Bri-tons free, Hap-py in Beef and Li - ber-ty.

THE SONG OF THE DAY.

Written by Brother THEODOSIUS FORREST.[*]

No more shall Fame expand her wings
To sound of heroes, states, and kings;
A nobler flight the Goddess takes,
To praise our British Beef in steaks,—
A joyful theme for Britons free,   } *Chorus after every*
Happy in Beef and Liberty.   }   *verse.*

Oh! charming Beef, of thee possest,
Completely carved in steaks, and dressed,
We taste the dear variety,
Produced in earth, in air, in sea,—
Their flavour's all combined in thee,
Fit for the sons of Liberty.

Throughout the realms where despots reign,
What tracks of glory now remain!
Their people, slaves of power and pride,
Fat Beef and Freedom are denied!
What realm, what state, can happy be,
Wanting our Beef and Liberty?

[*] Elected in the year 1763, and son of one of the original 24 Members in 1735.

O'er sea-coal fire and steel machine,
We broil the beauteous fat and lean ;
Our drink Oporto's grapes afford,
Whilst India's nectar crowns the board,—
A right repast for such as we,
Friends to good cheer and Liberty ! *

The usual Toast.

" Ne fidos inter amicos
Sit, qui dicta foras eliminet." †

* On singing the last chorus Members and Visitors joined hands all round.
† Motto over chimney-piece in dining-room.

The Nipperkin.

JUBILEE SONG.

25 February, 1786.

By Brother CHARLES MORRIS.

WHEN Freedom shook her vengeful shield
 In battle's wild commotion,
Her lightning scared the shattered field,
 Her thunder swept the ocean.
Resistless was the sacred rage
 That roused her soul to glory,
And hallowed is the deathless page
 That tells the Patriot's story.

Chorus.

In British breasts this spirit sprung
 For Freedom's preservation,
But British beef their sinews strung
 Who saved this freeborn nation.

When worth and wisdom led to fame,
 And civil virtue nourished,
When truth and faith adorned the name,
 And home-bred honour flourished,

Tyrannic faction baffled fled,
    Corruption fell confounded,
And Freedom reared her glorious head,
    By glorious hearts surrounded.
              Chorus.

When Reason loosed the shackled mind,
    And Priestcraft's night expired,
Here Science her rude works refin'd,
    Here Learning's sons retired.
'Twas here a Newton pierced the skies
    With bold unerring flight, sir ;
'Twas here the world saw Shakespeare rise,
    Its wonder and delight, sir.
              Chorus.

'Twas here, just fifty winters past,
    As on our leaf recited,
A few choice souls of social cast
    In friendship's bond united,
And warm'd with zeal that proudly gaz'd
    On England's better time, sir,
To Beef, the nerve of valour, rais'd
    An altar most sublime, sir.
              Chorus.

On Saturn's day this altar burns
    With festive preparation,
Where twice twelve Brothers rule by turns
    To pour a fit libation.

The Brethren flock you here behold,
   While with their welcome greeted,
And there the Father of the Fold *
   In honour justly seated.
                 Chorus.

Tho' sacred is our ox's rump,
   Old story will evince, sir,
If Fame deceive not with her trump,
   'Twas deified long since, sir.
To " Mithra's " bull all Persia bow'd,
   To " Apis " Egypt preach'd, sir.
To Baal's Calf whole countries vow'd,
   And Greece her "Boûs" beseeched, sir.
                 Chorus.

While thus we boast a general creed
   In honour of our shrine, sir,
You find the world long since agreed
   That Beef was food divine, sir.
And British fame still tells afar
   This truth, where'er she wanders,
For wine, for women, and for war,
   Beef steaks make Alexanders.
                 Chorus.

May Beef long bless this favoured coast,
   Where no despotic ruffian
Hath dared a Brazen Bull to roast
   With men alive for stuffing :

* Brother Richard Grindall, President on that day, and oldest Member of the Society.

Where never Jove, a tyrant god,
  Who loves fair maids to purloin,
Like a white bull the billows rode,
  With Madam on his sirloin.
                    Chorus.

Like Britain's Island lies our Steak,
  A sea of gravy bounds it ;
Shalots, profusely scattered, make
  The rock-work which surrounds it.
Your Isle's best emblem there behold,
  Remember ancient story ;
Be like your grandsires, rough and bold,
  And live and die with glory.
                    Chorus.

THE TOPER'S APOLOGY.

By Brother CHARLES MORRIS.

I 'M often ask'd by plodding souls,
  And men of crafty tongue,
What joy I find in draining bowls,
  And tippling all night long.
Now, though these cautious knaves I scorn,
  For once I'll not disdain
To tell them why I sit till morn,
  And fill my glass again.

'Tis by the glow my bumper gives
  Life's picture's mellow made ;
The fading light then brightly lives,
  And softly sinks the shade ;
Some happier tint still rises there
  With every drop I drain,—
And that I think 's a reason fair
  To fill my glass again.

My Muse, too, when her wings are dry,
  No frolic flight will take ;
But round a bowl she'll dip and fly,
  Like swallows round a lake.

Then, if the nymph will have her share
  Before she'll bless her swain,—
Why, that I think 's a reason fair
  To fill my glass again.

In life I've rung all changes, too,
  Run every pleasure down,—
Tried all extremes of Fancy through,
  And lived with half the town ;
For me there's nothing new or rare
  Till wine deceives my brain,—
And that I think 's a reason fair
  To fill my glass again.

Then, many a lad I liked is dead,
  And many a lass grown old ;
And as the lesson strikes my head,
  My weary heart grows cold.
But wine, awhile, holds off despair,
  Nay, bids a hope remain,—
And that I think 's a reason fair
  To fill my glass again.

Then, hipp'd and vex'd at England's state,
  In these convulsive days,
I can't endure the ruin'd fate
  My sober eye surveys ;
But, midst the bottle's dazzling glare,
  I see the gloom less plain,—
And that I think 's a reason fair
  To fill my glass again.

I find, too, when I stint my glass,
  And sit with sober air,
I'm prosed by some dull reasoning ass,
  Who treads the path of care ;
Or, harder taxed, I'm forced to hear
  Some coxcomb's fribbling strain,—
And that I think 's a reason fair
  To fill my glass again.

Nay, don't we see love's fetters, too,
  With different holds entwine?
While nought but death can some undo,
  There are some give way to wine.
With me, the lighter head I wear
  The lighter hangs the chain,—
And that I think 's a reason fair
  To fill my glass again.

And now I'll tell, to end my song,
  At what I most repine :
This cursed war, or right or wrong,
  Is war against all wine ;
Nay, port, they say, will soon be rare
  As juice of France or Spain,—
And that I think 's a reason fair
  To fill my glass again.

.

CONTRAST.

By Brother CHARLES MORRIS.

BETWEEN two eyes I must expire,
　My heart is gone, I own—
A black one sets it all on fire,
　A blue one melts it down :
There's lightning in the black one's glance,
　A sunbeam in the blue ;
One strikes it like a piercing lance,
　And one steals gently through.

By fire or water, then, it goes,
　But which I'm yet to learn—
At morn it burns, at night it flows,
　And flames and weeps by turn.
One piercer or one melter I
　Could face, and never quake ;
But two to one my powers defy—
　No battle I can make.

Singly, I own, I've often sparr'd
  With hazel and with jet ;
And, though by half a score hit hard,
  I've not been vanquished yet.
With one I'd fight its utmost art,
  Though light or dark its hue ;
But set on thus by both, my heart
  Is beaten black and blue.

THE CATALOGUE.

By Brother CHARLES MORRIS.

OH! that's what you mean now—a bit of a song;
    Why, faith, then, here goes, you shan't bother me long;
I require no teazing, no praying, or stuff:
By my soul! if you wish it, I'm ready enough;
To give you your end, you shall have a beginning;
And troth, though the music be not very fine,
It's a bit of a thing that a body may sing,
Just to set us a-going, and season our wine.

Oh! I once was a lover like some of you here,
And could feed a whole night on a sigh or a tear;
No sunshine I knew but from Kitty's black eye,
And the world was a desert when she wasn't by;
But, the devil knows how, I got fond of Miss Betty,
And Kitty slipp'd out of this bosom of mine;—
It's a bit of a thing that a body may sing,
Just to set us a-going, and season our wine.

The S. S. B. S.

Now Betty had eyes soft and blue as the sky,
And the lily was black when her bosom was by.
Oh ! I found I was fixed, and for ever her own,
Sure I was, soul and body were Betty's alone ;
But a sudden red shot from the golden-hair'd Lucy
Burnt Betty quite out, with a flame more divine ;—
It's a bit of a thing that a body may sing,
Just to set us a-going, and season our wine.

Now Lucy was stately, majestic, and tall,
And in feature and shape what a goddess you'd call ;
I adored, and I vowed if she'd not a kind eye,
I'd give up the whole world, and in banishment die ;
But Nancy came by, a round, plump little creature,
And fix'd in my heart quite another design ;—
It's a bit of a thing that a body may sing,
Just to set us a-going, and season our wine.

Little Nance, like a Hebe, was buxom and gay,
Had a bloom like a rose, and was fresher than May ;
Oh ! I felt if she frown'd I must die by a rope,
Or my bosom would burst if she slighted my hope ;
But the slim, taper, elegant Fanny look'd at me,
And truth, I no longer for Nancy could pine ;—
It's a bit of a thing that a body may sing,
Just to set us a-going, and season our wine.

Now Fanny's light frame was so slender and fine
That she skimm'd in the air like a shadow divine ;
Her motion bewitch'd, and to my loving eye
'Twas an angel soft gliding 'twixt earth and the sky.
'Twas all mighty well till I saw her fat sister,
And that gave a turn I could never define ;—
It's a bit of a thing that a body may sing,
Just to set us a-going, and season our wine.

Oh ! so I go on, ever constantly blest,
For I find I've a great store of love in my breast ;
And it never grows less—for whenever I try
To get one in my heart, I get two in my eye.
To all sorts of beauty I bow with devotion,
And all kinds of liquor by turns I make mine ;—
So I'll finish the thing, that another may sing,
Just to keep us a-going, and season our wine.

LAUGH WHILE YOU MAY.

By Brother CHARLES MORRIS.

THREE score and ten is the age of us men,
  And to many a period of trouble ;
But, merry and gay, I have laughed it away,
  And play'd, like a boy, with the bubble.
With a kiss and a cup I have kept my heart up,
  Each in turn, as kind fate would confer it ;
And, now kissing's done, I'll take two cups for one,
  And comfort the flesh with the spirit.

Let them rail who think fit, at my ways or my wit,
  I reply to the foes of good living,
" Heaven bade me be gay—to enjoy's to obey,
  And mirth is my prayer of thanksgiving."
When the crabbed with spleen would o'ershadow life's scene,
  I light up a spark to dispel it ;
And if snarlers exclaim, "What's this laughing fool's name?"
  Next verse of my ballad will tell it.

I'm a brat of old Horace—the song-scribbling Morris,
   More noted for rhyme than for reason;
One who roars and carouses, makes noise in all houses,
   And takes all good things in their season.
To this classic of joy, I became when a boy
   A pupil most ardent and willing;
And through life as a man, I've stuck fast to this plan,
   And passed it in flirting and filling.

They say, Laugh and grow fat, and that Care kills a cat,
   Though nine are the lives of poor Tabby.
As to Care, we all know a good stomach's its foe,
   And I've heartily fed from a baby.
Though Nature, it's said, need but salad and bread,
   I own I'm a flesh-loving sinner;
And nothing, I think, my gay spirits could sink,
   But skinning a flint for my dinner.

Old Lucullus, they say, fifty cooks had each day,
   And Vitellius's meal cost a million;
Now my stomach's as good—what or where be my food,
   In a chop-house or Royal Pavilion.
At all meals, if enough, I most happily stuff,
   And a song from my heart alike rushes,
Though I've not fed my lungs upon nightingale's tongues,
   Or the brains of goldfinches and thrushes.

The S. S. B. S.

Every mortal, we find, is more placid and kind,
    When the stomach's relieved from its craving,
E'en the sour and the dull yield a smile when they're full,
    And the cunning's lest bent on be-knaving.
After dinner, men best grant a boon or request;
    That's the hour for asking and suing;
And with ladies I've found, through my life's giddy round,
    It's the very best moment for wooing.

But all stomach, they say, in true love goes away
    From a delicate languishing swainer;
Now I never found cause yet to shut up my jaws,
    Though my heart has been pierced like a strainer.
Poets best too, it's said, write and sing when unfed;
    But if starved I'm undone head and throttle;
For the pot and the spit are the source of my wit,
    And the fount of my fancy the bottle.

When my eyes take a gaze through the whims of my days,
    And the glass gilds the passing illusion,
What soul more on earth feels the spur of wild mirth,
    Or glows with more social effusion?
Round my old head of snow my life's spring seems to glow,
    Though joys into visions be dwindled;
And, though faded the truth, I'm bewitched into youth,
    And my heart's faded embers new kindled.

Then I'll take t'other sup, while the ashes light up,—
 The spark, at my age, must be sprinkled;
Folly holds it a sin to grow cold and grow thin,
 Though wisdom sit frozen and wrinkled.
As in youth, when best fed, I'd best strength, heart, and head,
 My old days with good cheer I still cherish;
And while healthy they run with good feeding and fun,
 Skin-and-grief may preach on till they perish.

Oh! whatever fate bring, too much thought's a bad thing,
 Neither good for the blood nor the temper;
Deep reflections apply a sad film to the eye,
 And throw the fair world in distemper.
Each breast, in its days, has some sunshiny rays,
 Sweet blossoms of life in fair weather,—
Then let Sympathy strike on all bosoms alike,
 And let us be happy together.

THE BIRTHDAY.

By Brother CHARLES MORRIS.

TIME'S mark'd a year more on my tally;
　　But mark'd with the finger of mirth,
And left, what in life I most value,
　　The friends who now honour my birth.
But how shall so humble a poet
　　A boon so distinguish'd repay?
Can my pen with due gratitude show it?
　　Or tongue tell the pride of this day?

Upheld by this kind estimation,
　　High cheer'd by the grace of this board,
My strength seems renew'd in creation,
　　My age to youth's spirits restored.
I waive what I long had intended——
　　My time-wasted Muse to dismiss;
And proudly and sweetly befriended,
　　I hold her for moments like this.

In youth, if my song I gave over,
   Fresh charms from the fair or the flask,
Still won back the toper or lover,
   And spurr'd the warm Muse to her task:
And now, when Time bids me retire,
   And Fancy's dim light's a mere gleam,
The spark is fresh flush'd into fire
   By rays that from Royalty beam.

Thus Flaccus sung gayer and faster,
   By favour Imperial inspired,
A smile from the lip of Rome's master
   Still gave him fresh life when he tired.
But in love, or the joys of the table,
   He ran a short course upon earth;
He lived not to play with Life's fable,
   Like me through a century's mirth.

But, ah! what I owe this preceptor!
   I trod in his steps, and was blest:
The hand that sustains Britain's sceptre
   Long lifted my Muse and caressed:
And now, when the spade waits to ground me,
   And gloominess darkens my day,
The glory of Brunswick shines round me,
   And bids me still bask in its ray.

While I see, in the friends who now meet me,
  How favour and fervour unite ;
How Royalty deigns here to greet me ;
  How hearts mellow round me to-night :
Oh ! judge what I feel 'midst this pleasure,
  That shows I yet hold upon earth
A heart worthy Friendship's sweet treasure,
  A Muse ever welcome to Mirth !

High charmed, through a day beyond prizing,
  With full tide of spirit in play,
I feel while its joys I'm revising,
  My soul's had its revel to-day.
Then take, my illustrious protector,
  Dear friends, take, since now we must part,
Oh, take, in this brimmer of Nectar,
  The full-flowing thanks of my heart !

THE END OF THE COURSE.

By Brother CHARLES MORRIS.

TIME bids me dismount from my hobby;
   Indeed, he has run a long race:
And it's owned in the field and the lobby,
   My pony was fleet in his pace.
Perhaps I have spurr'd him too freely,
   And not used the curb as I should;
But e'en when he swerved and was reely,
   He still showed a bit of good blood.

Now sunk, like the high-mettled racer,
   The great public turf he forsakes;
But in private is still a brisk racer,
   And starts with good will for the Steaks;
There no crossing we ever discover,
   No blacklegged treachery's played:
There the course is still fairly run over,
   The jockey still honestly weighed.

But now to have done with allusions,
  And name my best joys and best ends,
'Tis to find that my cheerful effusions
  Are stamped with the seal of my friends ;
That my efforts for mirth and for pleasure
  Produce what they strive to sustain,—
That they listen with joy to my measure,
  And trust to my Fancy again.

This still prompts my Muse to her duty,
  This wakes the warm zeal of my heart ;
Guides the Fancy in efforts for Beauty,
  And colours each sketch of her art :
'Tis so sweet a reward to my spirit,
  So grateful a charm to my ear,
That, eager the blessing to merit,
  I run with delight my career.

And while I hear praise that thus pleases,
  My Muse her gay toil will prolong ;
When the day shall arrive that it ceases,
  That day is the last of my song :
And fast the weak moment advances
  When Fate's measured justice shall say,
" The night must now close on his fancies ;
  The merry old dog's had his day ! "

WOO'D AND MARRIED AN 'AW.

By Brother CHARLES MORRIS.

YOU know the tune of the song
    Call'd, Woo'd and marry'd, an 'aw ;
Then, help my chorus along,
    For my voice isn't worth a straw.
I'm now in a cue to sing,
    If you'll but join my lay;
For I've dipped my Muse's wing,
    And she's ready to rise and play.

Chorus.

Then, guests, and brothers, an 'aw,
    Brothers, and guests, an 'aw,
Oh, lend a lift to my lilt, then,
    Guests, and brothers, an 'aw.

I feel my spirits get up,
    And joy dance round my heart;
I'm better for every cup,
    And I warrant I'll play my part.
Gay visions steal o'er my brain,
    My fancy grows warm and free,
Then help to sweeten my strain,
    And you never shall flag for me.

Chorus.

The S. S. B. S.

Some folks will grumble, and cry
   That earth grows nothing but care ;
But what do they mean, say I,
   When the myrtle and vine are there ?
The ups and downs of the world,
   Are frolics of Fate's decree ;
Our heads were made to be whirl'd,
   So a whirlabout life for me.
                    Chorus.

To seize all moments of mirth,
   That brighten the shades of Fate,
Is man's sweet duty on earth,
   However the spleen may prate.
A chequer of gloom and glee
   Is the life that the gods provide ;
And an impious fool is he
   Who snarls at the changing tide.
                    Chorus.

I argue with no grave men,
   Nor mope with reasoning folks ;
If life be a farce, what then ?
   It's filled with very good jokes.
While whisking about I'm found,
   If health in the circle be,
However the world goes round,
   It's a merry-go-round for me.
                    Chorus.

The Bard of my early youth,
 The tutor of Love's sweet day,
Well taught the lesson of truth,
 That a man should be pleased and gay.
By this cherishing light I teach,
 Which bright in my glass I see;
And they who in shade will preach,
 May go to the shades for me.
       Chorus.

If you wish for a certain cure
 To cut out the thorns of life,
There isn't a cut more sure
 Than the cut of the Beef-Steak knife:
For a cordial is mingled there
 That ever will cure afford,
In the brotherly love we bear,
 And the charms of the cheerful board.
       Chorus.

In every ill that falls,
 Or shadow that clouds our way,
The sunshine within those walls,
 Still brightens the darkest day.
An age hath its lustre play'd
 To mellow the fruits of Joy:
And never may blight or shade
 These sweetest of fruits destroy!
       Chorus.

EPITAPH ON EDWARD HEARDSON,

MANY YEARS COOK TO THE BEEF-STEAK SOCIETY.

By Brother CHARLES MORRIS.

H IS last steak done, his fire raked out and dead,
    Dish'd for the worms himself, lies honest Ned.
We, who partook of all his fleshly toils,
Received his bastings, too, and shar'd his broils,
Now in our turn a mouthful carve and trim,
And dress at Phœbus' fire our steak for him.
His heart, which well deserved a noble grave,
Was grateful, patient, modest, just, and brave,*
And ne'er did Earth's wide maw a morsel gain
Of kindlier juices or more tender grain.
His tongue where duteous friendship humbly dwelt,
Charmed all who heard the faithful zeal he felt.
Still, to whatever end his chops he moved,
'Twas all well-season'd, relished and approved.
This room his heav'n ! when threat'ning fate drew nigh,
And death's chill shade had dimm'd his ling'ring eye,
His fondest hopes, betrayed with many a tear,
Were that his life's last spark might glimmer here ;
And the last words that choked his parting sigh,—†
" Oh, at your feet, dear masters, let me die ! "

* He was a renowned and expert pugilist.
† One of the last wishes of this faithful servant was that he might be removed into the room of the Society, and that he should die contented there.

RETIREMENT OF THE BARD.

FROM AUTOGRAPH LETTER.

LONDON, *May* 18, 1831.

MY DEAR FRIEND :

Being now on the verge of ninety years of age, and thus disqualified for all future participation in the pleasures of gaiety, and precluded, moreover, by a cruel change of circumstances from all wish to carry a depressed spirit beyond the limits of my own threshold, I have, from the double necessity of this time-worn incapacity and diminution of the means of enjoyment, taken leave of all worldly festivity, to close my life in humble retirement and domestic privacy ; but, that I may not be as wholly lost in remembrance as I am in worldly intercourse, I have taken the liberty of addressing a few parting words from my Muse, to the beloved brethren I shall see no more, and I beg you, as the worthy Father of the amiable Society, to have the goodness to offer it to their perusal, with the sincere regard, respect and best wishes of

> Your Affectionate Friend and
> Most obedt. humble Servant,
> CHAS. MORRIS.

J. RICHARDS, Esq.

This 18th of May being the Birthday on which I enter my Eighty-sixth year, I thought it a fit moment for enclosing you my little valedictory scrap.

A PARTING WORD

TO MY BELOVED BRETHREN OF THE OLD BEEF-STEAK SOCIETY.

ADIEU to the world ! where I gratefully own
  Few men more delight or more comfort have known ;
To an age far beyond mortal lot have I trod
The path of pure health, that best blessing of God ;
And so, mildly devout, Nature tempered my frame,
Holy Patience still soothed, when adversity came :
Thus, with mind ever cheerful, and tongue never tir'd,
I sung the gay strains these sweet blessings inspired,
And by blending light mirth with a moral-mix'd stave,
Won the smile of the gay and the nod of the grave.
But at length the dull languor of mortal decay
Throws a weight on a spirit too light for its clay,
And, the fancy subdued as the body's oppress'd,
Resigns the faint flights that scarce wake in the breast ;
A painful memento, that man's not to play
A game of light folly through life's sober day :
A just admonition, though viewed with regret,
Still blessedly offered but thanklessly met.
Too long I perhaps like the many who stray,
Have upheld the gay themes of the Bacchanal's day ;
But at length time has brought, what it ever will bring,
A gloom that excites more to sigh than to sing.

In this close of life's chapter, ye high favoured few,
Take my Muse's last tribute—this painful adieu :
Take my wish, that your bright social circle on earth
For ever may flourish in concord and mirth :
For the long years of joy I have shared at your board,
Take the thanks of my heart, where they long have been stored ;
And remember, when Time tolls my last parting knell,
The Old Bard dropt a tear, and then bade ye farewell.

C. M.

May 18, 1831.

EXTRACT FROM THE MINUTES OF THE SOCIETY,
MAY 19, 1832.

" The Old Bard, Captain Charles Morris, having entered his eighty-seventh year, and being in full possession of health, and of those splendid lyrical talents which have charmed this Sublime Society for more than half a century, again took his seat at the board.

" The deep gratification of such an event could not be permitted to pass unnoticed, and the Sublime Society requested, as a favour, that the following recent effort of his Muse should be recorded— the Sublime Society desiring to possess, in the first instance, one of those effusions of his genius, which, when published to the world hereafter, will give immortality to his name, illustrate the lyrical poetry of England, and place it in the annals of fame with the Odes of Horace."

LAST SONG OF THE OLD BARD.

WELL, I'm come, my good friends, your kind wish to obey,
   To sing, if I can, a last song here to-day ;
To turn the heart's sighs to the throbbings of joy,
And a grave aged man to a merry old boy.

'Tis a bold transformation ! a daring design,
But not past the power of friendship and wine ;
And I trust that e'en yet this sweet mixture will raise
A brisk spark of light on the shade of my days.

The swan, it is said by the poets, still tries
To sing, if he can, a last song ere he dies,
So I'll try, my dear friends, tho' for such an old man,
Th' attempt savours more of the goose than the swan.

When I look round the board, and recall to my breast,
How *long* here I sat and how *long* I was blest ;
In a mingled effusion that steals to my eyes,
I sob o'er the wishes that life now denies.

'Twas here my youth, manhood, and age used to pass,
Till Time bad me mark the low sands in his glass;
Then, with grief that alone death can hide from my view,
I gave up the blessing and sadly withdrew.

But my sorrow it soothes, my dear friends, let me say,
As your Tribute of Friendship I proudly survey,
That my heart can yet glow with the joy it reveals,
And my tongue has yet power to tell what it feels.

How many bright spirits I've seen disappear,
While Fate's lucky lot held me happily here ;
How many kind hearts and gay bosoms gone by,
That oft left me to mingle my mirth with a sigh.

But whate'er be the lot, that life's course may afford,
Or howe'er Fate may chequer this ever lov'd board,
So the memory of Pleasure brings sorrow relief,
That a ray of past joy ever gleams o'er my grief.

And still in your presence, more brightly it glows,—
Here high mount my spirits where always they rose ;
Here a sweet mingled vision of Present and Past
Still plays in my sight, and will play to the last.

When my spirits are low, for relief and delight
I still place your splendid memorial * in sight,
And call to my Muse when care strives to pursue,—
Bring the Steaks to my fancy and Bowl to my view.

When brought, at its sight all the blue-devils fly,
And a world of gay visions rise bright to the eye ;
Cold Fear shuns the cup where warm memory glows,
And grief, shamed by joy, hides his budget of woes.

* A large and elegant silver bowl, with an appropriate inscription, presented· by the Society, as a testimonial of affectionate esteem.

'Tis a pure holy fount ! where, for ever, I find
A sure double charm for the body and mind ;
For I feel while I'm cheered by the drop that I lift,
I'm blest by the motive that hallows the gift.

Then take, my dear friends, my best thanks and my praise,
For a boon that thus comforts and honours my days.
And permit me to say, as there's life in a bowl,
That Taste forms its body, but Friendship its soul.

ODE,

ON THE SUBLIME SOCIETY REMOVING FROM THE LYCEUM TAVERN TO THE BEDFORD COFFEE HOUSE, 7 JANUARY, 1832.

By Brother R. B. PEAKE.

OH ! what is that crowd in the Strand, sir?
    And what is this bustle so strange ?
And why does that large waggon stand, sir,
Where once stood fam'd Exeter 'Change !
Oh ! what are those oak chairs and tables,
Those pieces of meat in large lumps?
They're the S. S. B. S.'s move-ables,
The Steaks are removing their rumps.

There's a mitre, a sword, and a gridiron,
A night-cap, an apron, and sheet,
A serjeant, a halbert, (a high one)
Confounding the mob in the street.
There's the grate that so long o'er the embers
Held its place.   All are ready to start ;
So lift in the twenty-four members,
And pack them all safe in the cart.

On the top of the cart, the Recorder *
Was busy in spite of his gout,
To keep the procession in order,
And see the Society out.

         * Brother Richards.

With a prattle, as usual inclin'd, he
Kept up in a disjointed chat ;
"Out of court these damned fellows won't mind me,
So pitch up my three-cornered hat."

Sir Andrew * is stowed tight and merry,
Sir Ronald † is shaken about,
Hold fast by your seat, Knight of Kerry,
For members are often thrown out.
Wait a moment, I've left out a fat one,
Who plenty of steaks can absorb,—
As Lonsdale the painter is that one,
We've christened him BEEF À LA DAUB.

To the Bedford away quickly take us :
(A voice swore) " I'll not go, I vow."
Said Hallett, " 'Mongst twenty-four steakers,
Pray ' what can the matter be ' now ? "
It's only our jolly old Bishop,‡
Let us join in a general prayer ;
(As we all his new house quickly wish up)
We soon may be carted back there.

Two dozen choice boys in a waggon,
Who would not be taken alive,
But before it was settled to drag on
It was asked, "Who is sober, to drive ? "
Says Heath, "I'm acquainted with all town :
Pray fix upon me as the man."
But the Brethren deputed Lord Saltoun,—
They knew that he'd oft led the van.

* Brother Barnard.　　　† Brother Fergusson.　　　‡ Brother Samuel Arnold.

I have gone on thus far, and am wary
To give no offence in my verse ;
But where is our good Secretary *
To sit with his Book and his purse ?
Could I speak of his diffidence ample,
Of his modesty could I impart
A grain for each member's example,
By George ! it would break down the cart.

Now, as all the live luggage was seated,
A whip made the old horses creep,
(With a whip we are now and then treated),
But Linley behind was asleep.
He waked, and upraising his finger,
" Stay, Travellers, prithee remain,
If you leave here your principal singer,
You will never wake music again."

Say, who is that tall, lanky fellow ?
Avast there, my hearties ! what cheer ?
It's only our Admiral so Yellow †
Who wants now the waggon to steer.
There's our Doctor ‡ from Chelsea, I mention, as
One for whom ministers pray,
For considerably thinning the pensioners,—
He kills nine or ten every day.

* Brother Henry Stephenson.   † Brother Dundas.   ‡ Brother Somerville.

SONG.

By Brother JAMES LONSDALE.

BEHOLD an old Painter, who labours in vain,
 To give his Steak friends but one atom of brain.
Nay, look round this room, and with Macbeth you'll cry,
The brains are all out but the men will not die.

> Derry down, &c.

Gaffer Walsh at the door like a Cerberus sits,
To scare the High Bailiff* quite out of his wits;
He damns his " Hark, hark," and he swears with a grin,
The High Bailiff's song was original sin.

> Derry down, &c.

Billy Linley hangs next, with his toothpick so gay,
That family plate he will always display ;
Then to Newgate he goes, with a tear in his eye,
And says, " My good friend, are you going to die ? "

> Derry down, &c.

* Brother Arthur Morris, High Bailiff of Westminster.

The Recorder* renowned, in his cock and pinch hat,
For trying offences and long-winded chat,
Six thousand a-year he is paid in hard gold,
For cracking his jokes full five hundred years old.
                         Derry down, &c.

Sammy Arnold, they say, when returning one night,
Put a poor Hackney coachman in terrible fright :
He opened the window, cried " D—— you, hallo ! "
When Jarvey jumped down and said, " How came you so ? "
                         Derry down, &c.

Sammy blustered and swore by his own precious eyes
That Jarvey should smart for his impudent lies ;
Besides, your poor horses you've put in a funk,
But Jarvey persisted the gemman was drunk.
                         Derry down, &c.

Brother Brougham, mind's a name I would fain keep from you,
But give me a freehold and I'll vote for the Blue ;
Each tint of the rainbow can mammon unfold,
Even blue turns to green when you touch it with gold.
                         Derry down, &c.

But to follow this prismatic system of mine,
True blue is the colour that's nearest divine,
And the Gods, when they painted their heavenly screen,
They swore they'd have nothing but ultra-marine.
                         Derry down, &c.

* Brother Richards.

The Corporal* next looks so gallant and gay,
But never would fight if he could run away.
Says he, " It's all stuff about powder and ball,—
Let me die the death of brave Governor Wall."

Derry down, &c.

There's Admiral Dundas, whom we've brought to the charge ;
He that once ploughed the ocean now plies a dung-barge:
Of those thundering ships he could not bear the smell,
So he now pipes all hands in the Regent's Canal.

Derry down, &c.

There's Jocky of Norfolk†, who merrily ran
His threescore and ten that's allotted to man,
Then died in the faith and true love of a Steaker,
Having drunk up his wine and spit out the wafer.

Derry down, &c.

The Bard of Old England‡ sits cocking his ear,
As if half afraid we should rival him here ;
For the secret's found out, that to make a good song,
Only fix on a tune that will help it along.

Derry down, &c.

Then there's our Lord Mayor§—that little black thing,
That kicked up a dust 'twixt the Queen and the King ;
He headed addresses of brazen-faced mobs,
He's employed by the City in all dirty jobs.

Derry down, &c.

---

* Brother General Sir Ronald Fergusson.   † Brother the Duke of Norfolk.
‡ Brother Captain Morris.   § Brother Sir Matthew Wood, M.P.

The next is a Duke,* whose ear is so good,
He could not bear the bass voice of Alderman Wood,
So he took from his pocket a jack-a-legs knife
And made him sing alt at the risk of his life.

> Derry down, &c.

Tho' last he's not least in my true sublime song,
Where Princes and Patriots cut jokes in a throng ;
That great Prince Augustus,† he never will wince—
The King was a Steaker when he was a Prince. ‡

> Derry down, &c.

---

* Brother the Duke of Leinster.   † Brother H. R. H. the Duke of Sussex.
‡ Brother H. R. H. the Prince of Wales, afterwards George IV.

SONG.

By Brother HENRY STEPHENSON.

I F you wish to hear me sing,
   Come listen to my ditty,
In the shape of a song ; tho' not very long,
   I hope you'll think it witty.

My subject is beef-eating
   At a place called the Lyceum,
By a motley crew of every hue :
   'Twould do you good to see 'em.

The first, Sir Andrew Barnard,*
   With him I will begin, sir,
He drinks no more at the gin-shop door,
   But he sups with Queen at Windsor.

Then next is Riversdale Grenfell,
   He is the son of Pascoe ;
He never fails to go to Wales,—
   We wish he'd go to Glasgow.

* Equerry to the Queen Dowager.

Then there is Sir John Hobhouse ;
  Who he is perhaps you'll ax us :
He was an M.P. who tried to be free,
  But was beat by the assessed taxes.

Then there sits Archibald Hastie :
  We'll take him in his turn, sir :
He'll get very frisky as he drinks his whisky
  Out of the bowl of Burns, sir.

Then there is John Lord Saltoun,
  He fought at Waterloo, sir ;
He charged with the Guards, and afterwards
  He helped the Horse Guards blue, sir.

And there is Dr. Somerville,
  His learning is amazing ;
For Mrs S. is an authoress,
  Much given to star-gazing.

And there is Jemmy Lonsdale,
  Who painted all our pictures ;
But his works of note are not worth a groat,
  If you read Sir Joshua's lectures.

And there is his son Edward,
  A Doctor, as he tells, sir ;
He physics all, both great and small,
  But he never makes them well, sir.

And there is George Dundas,
   He's a Captain in the Navy :
He got lost in the fogs near the Isle of Dogs,
   So we sent for Sir Humphry Davy.

And there's Sir Ronald Fergusson,
   One of the Military ;
He's a general bold, though not very old,
   And his head not over hairy.

Then there's John Benjamin Heath,*
   Who is a bank director ;
He is chief consul to the Great Mogul,
   Or some such malefactor.

And then there's Johnny Richards,
   Our Recorder he is styled ;
He can faster talk than he can walk,—
   We wish his tongue were filed.

Then there's the Hon. Fox Maule ;
   If folks have not defamed him,
He shod the horse at Charing Cross,
   Whereby they say he lamed him.

Then there's the Duke of Leinster—
   He is a very good fellow ;
He is the only Duke in Ireland's nook,
   And he plays on the Violoncello.

* Baron Heath, Consul-General for Italy.

Then next comes Sammy Arnold,
   The landlord of our room, sir :
We pay him rent for what is lent,
   And quite enough, thinks Brougham, sir.

Then there is his son Walter,
   He is a little nice man ;
He's here and there and everywhere,
   And he lives next door to Wiseman.

*Then last is Henry Stephenson,
   Who uses strong expressions ;
He's very true to buff and blue,
   And was born in tights and hessians.

*He is our worthy Treasurer;
   His jokes he never ends 'em ;
But the worst of his quips are his damnable whips,
   And the Lord knows how he spends 'em.

* These two verses were added by Brother Tom Arnold.

ADDRESS TO BROTHER BROUGHAM,

THE LORD HIGH CHANCELLOR OF ENGLAND.

By Brother C. W. HALLETT.

TO BE SUNG IN FULL CHORUS.

FROM the most Sublime Society, at a very numerous meeting,
To the Lord High Chancellor of England, these come greeting!
Whereas it has pleased His Majesty King William, in his great
    benignity,
To raise your Lordship to this most exalted dignity,
We, your Brethren in Beef, do heartily felicitate you thereupon,
And rejoice to behold you sitting old Eldon's chair upon.
Tho' many Chancellors in *Wigs* we've seen before ye,
A Whig Chancellor is a much more uncommon thing than a Tory:
For time out of mind the Tories have had all their wishes,
And have not only been Masters of the *Rolls* but also of the loaves
    and fishes.

> Alteration! Alteration!
> What a wonderful alteration!

Yet pray forget not, in your present elevation,
You owe it all to having gained a station
In this Sublime and Worshipful Society,
Which shines with talents in immense variety!

Your crude notions of Equity would ne'er have been reduced to
    any order,
But for the valuable lessons you have had from our learned
    Recorder.
Tho' you've some fluency of speech from copying *Lewin's* garrulity,
Yet to believe you an orator requires all Billy *Linley's* credulity.
Gravity you've borrowed from *Stephenson*, Wit from *Arthur Morris*,
Wisdom from *Alderman Wood*, and modesty from the *Knight of*
    Kerry;
While your graceful mien was given on *Lonsdale's* Easel,
Who paints every body, as the song says, very "like a weasel."

                Alteration, &c.

In brief, and much to Briefs you own yourself a debtor ;
But Chancery *suits* will *suit* you now much better,
For now no longer you have an estate in *fee*,
As Barristers' Estates are wont to be.
Tho' you have not become first singer at the French Opera,*
(Which, after all, would have been an appointment much more
    properer,)
And may not choose to sing La "Pipe de Tabac,"† or smoke a pipe
    of short-cut,
'Tis pretty plain, at all events, that we've a *Pipe of Port* got
We'll file the Bill : You'll only have to pay it :
Put in your answer : will you dare gainsay it ?

                Alteration, &c.

* See Memoir, p. 26.
† The only song Brother Brougham was ever known to have sung, at least at the S. S. B. S.

So now we'll drink your health, and promise ye, if 'tis no treason,
You shall be drunk again each Saturday night throughout the
    season :
For if we cannot on the Gridiron roast ye,
At least in Bumpers large and deep we'll toast ye ;
We'll laud your Judgments, Orders, and Injunctions,
And swear you admirably perform your functions.
We wish you all honour, dignities and riches,
And health to wear out your new pair of checkered breeches.
Nay, more, if faction don't your party root out,
We wish your reign in Chancery long enough to wear a whole *suit*
    out.

Alteration, &c.

STEAK SONG.

By Brother C. W. Hallett.

YOU ask me to sing, and each Brother, 'tis said,
   A song must produce of his own proper head.
You must take no offence, for there's nought will be seen in
Whatever I say that can boast any meaning.
For want of a subject, I'll try to rehearse you
What other good Steakers in singing have done ;
   It will do very well as a body may tell,
   Just to set us a-going and season our fun.

Brother *Linley* sings Dibden and Purcell and Locke,
And of modern composers he hates all the stock ;
He gives us " Stay, Traveller, tarry the night,"
Till some of us tarry away in a fright.
But Corporal *Ferguson* sings it much better,
And all his fine graces and quirks has outdone.
                    But he does very well, &c.

This Corporal bold is a singer most chaste,
He's deficient in nothing but voice, ear, and taste ;

He laments he's no voice, and grieves for it all day,
But the truth is his voices are all at Kircaldie.
Their influence sweet, tho' a soldier, he relishes
More than the sound of a trumpet or gun.
But he does very well, &c.

There's Alderman *Wood* used to sing rather gruffly,
Till the fierce Duke of *Leinster* once handled him roughly,
Who, thinking the change was a surgical duty,
Soon made him sing alto like Signor Velluti.
He now warbles forth a delightful soprano,
As soft as the tones of a delicate Nun.
And he does very well, &c.

This same Duke of *Leinster*, when once it was known
That we all were to scribble a song of our own,
Determined to stay all the summer in London,
On purpose, by fagging, to try and get *one done*.
No longer he sings of the pigs and the praties,
Tho' of noble St. Patrick a genuine son.
But he does very well, &c.

Our jolly Recorder,* a lame one we find him,
Cries out for more pay, but we none of us mind him,
And lays down the law in his three-cornered castor,
Which has more point than anything said by its master.
He pretends to have read all Blackstone's Commen*ta*ries,—
I believe in my conscience he never read one.
But he does very well, &c.

* Brother John Richards.

There's Manager *Arnold*, I'll tell you his way ;
He rejects, with disdain, some poor author's first play,
But reserves all the jokes that are pointed or witty,
And dishes them up in his own meagre ditty.
He knows very well if he trusts his invention
His productions will have but a moderate run.
But he does very well, &c.

There's *Lonsdale*, who daubed all these signs round the room,
From the Prince at the top down to Counsellor *Brougham*,
Kindly tells us in verse, which to Grub Street he went for,
The names of the Worthies his portraits are meant for.
Without such an index e'en *Stephenson's* tinder-box
Ne'er would such great admiration have won.
But he does very well, &c.

This *Stephenson*, too, deals in doggerel sublime,
At nothing he sticks to accomplish a rhyme ;
His song, like his talk, labours hard to be witty,
But he always stops short in the midst of his ditty.
When verses are lame 'tis no wonder they halt, sir,
And that is the truth, so you'll pardon the pun.
It will do very well, &c.

Brother *Terry* sings bass—the High Bailiff sings small,
And the famed Knight of *Kerry*, he don't sing at all.
Friend *Lewin's* sweet pipe we shall ne'er I hope lack,
It is only excelled by " La Pipe de Tabac."

In English, we know, that *Brougham* can't ever speak,
So no wonder the language in singing he'd shun,
>> But he does very well, &c.

There's *Hobhouse*, who comes with true Brotherly hate,
And damns all his Brothers, both little and great,
Such a Reprobate be that his blessings would damn,
So each damn is a blessing that comes from *John Cam*.
He would sing them, but, shocked at his impious rhyming,
Our Bard, who was asked for a tune, would give none.
>> But he does very well, &c.

But what shall I say of our mighty Old Bard,
Whose genius we worship with pious regard !
The presumption of Phaëton, sure, must be mine,
To but hang on the wheels of his chariot divine.
But pri'thee don't smother my poor little taper,
Because you're enjoying the blaze of the sun.
>> It will do very well, &c.

BEEF AND LIBERTY.

By Brother C. W. HALLETT.

THERE are four-and-twenty Steakers on the Rota !
   And there's John *Richards*, the renowned Recorder of our
      Society,
Who lectures us for all our sins, the most heinous of which is the
      sin of sobriety !
And there's Billy *Linley*, who, in his anxiety to court the Graces,
Whenever he's singing twists his ugly mug into all sorts of queer
      grimaces.
And there's *Lonsdale* the painter, who understands his business
      so ill,
The landlord would not trust him to paint the Saracen's Head on
      Snow Hill.
And there's Tommy *Lewin*, who looks as solemn and as sober as
      any Parish Vicar,
But in reality drinks like a fish, and very much the same sort of
      liquor.
Then there's *Arnold*, who kept a theatre and let us a room in the
      centre in't,
But as all his Ladies' dressing-rooms were there, at first we didn't
      like to enter in't.

And there's Lord *Saltoun,* with a voice as soft and melodious as
    any young spinster,
One would think he'd been attended by our famous operator the
    Duke of *Leinster.*
And then there's the Duke himself, whose surgical skill to ad-
    vance, it
Ought to have at least forty good pages of panegyric in the
    Lancet.
And there's his jolly namesake, the knight of *Kerry,* we're always
    glad to see his face again,
Who dreamt one night that he was a Lord of the Treasury, but
    before he waked in the morning he was out of place again—
        This is our jolly Saturday,
        Therefore we will be merry.

Then there's General *Johnson,* who the old Gridiron has very
    nearly forsaken ;
But he comes up once a year just to show himself and save his
    bacon.
There's *Hobhouse,* too, has been a bit of a truant ; he prefers to
    mob it,
And dine at the Crown and Anchor for the sake of meeting his
    dear friend *Cobbett.*
And there's the renowned and patriotic Sir Francis *Burdett,*
If he has ever been here above once these two years I never heard it.
There's *Whitbread,* if he doesn't come himself sends his porter here
    to us,
And we all like him too well to wish he should come with his Bier
    to us !

There's Sir Andrew *Barnard*, better known among us as Sir Andrew
· Bombard,
Who sings a mighty comical Irish ditty, which must have been
written by a rum bard.
There's Dickey *Peake*, who is a manufacturer of *damned* good
Farces ;
Some call him the devil's Peak, but nobody says that Peake an
ass is.
And there's our new elected member, Walter *Campbell* of Islay,
Who made a long speech one night, and, to say the truth, spoke it
most vilely.
And *Heath*, who wears such thundering whiskers, tho' his beauty's
rather on the wane, sir,
That some call him Bushey Heath, some Black Heath, and some
call him Salisbury Plain, sir.
This is our jolly Saturday,
Therefore we will be merry.

Then there's Lord Chancellor *Brougham*, who for want of some-
thing to do, turned maker of Almanacks one day,
But the very first year was puzzled to tell us which was Easter
Sunday.
And there's Dr. *Somerville*, who is an M.D. and not a D.D.,
And the summit of his ambition is to succeed to the practice of
Dr. Eady.
And then there's Corporal *Ferguson*, with a head as bald as ever it
can be,
Who sits to *Lonsdale* whenever he has a sign to paint of the
Marquis of Granby.

And there's the brave Admiral *Dundas*, we never had such a Lord
    of the Admiralty as him afore ;
His place is to sit all day at 'the top of the House and pull the
    strings of the semaphore.
And there's his nephew, the Honourable *John*, we have only lately
    elected him :
I shall tell you when he says anything funny, but as yet I haven't
    detected him.
And then there's Harry *Stephenson*, our unconscionable Secretary,
Who makes heavy whips to pay for Cheeses and other nice things
    he sends to Lady Mary.
And " tho' last not least in our dear love " is our Royal Brother,
    Prince *Augustus*,*
Who cuts his joke as freely as his beef and makes us laugh enough
    to burst us.
So now I think you'll allow of names I've given you plenty
But I must just mention Number One to make the number four-
    and-twenty.
          This is our jolly Saturday,
          Therefore we will be merry.

* Brother H. R. H. the Duke of Sussex.

SONG.

By Brother SAMUEL JAMES ARNOLD.

FOR HIS SON (AND BROTHER) WALTER ARNOLD.

I HAVE heard of a Bard,* who for many a year
   Was the life and the soul of the friends who meet here ;
I have heard of his wit, and his song, and his whim,
But, alas ! for poor me, I have never heard him.
Derry down, &c.

Aye, "down derry down," as 'tis said he once sang,
In his splendid old age, though in vigour still young ;
And Curran, I'm told, cried in eloquent truth,—
" E'en die when you will, Bard, you'll die in your youth."
Derry down, &c.

And truly he spoke, tho' I scarce can allow
The immortal Old Bard has proved mortal e'en now :
While the Bays that encircled his time-honoured head
Still flourish and live—sure the bard is not dead.
Derry down, &c.

* Brother Charles Morris.

But if, in sad truth, that bright spirit has flown,
And of mirth, song, and wit has vacated the throne,—
Sure at this social board, though with sorrow o'ercast,
His memory lives and will live to the last.

Derry down, &c.

Yes, yes, though in grief we this measure rehearse,
That hovering spirit still dictates my verse !
Of his genius sublime, though I claim not a part,
It blossoms and lives in each Beef-Steaker's heart.

Derry down, &c.

For when Father Time cropp'd the fruits and the flowers
Of the joyous old man who embellished your hours,
He left us this record, " While *I* live, be sure
The name of Charles Morris like me shall endure."

Derry down, &c.

I dare not presume for a moment to guess
How my lay will be felt by the S.S.B.S.;
But this I declare, and I speak by the card,
I would give half a life to have heard your Old Bard.

Derry down, &c.

THE VISITORS' SONG.

By W. JERDAN, Esq.

HOW lucky the wight whose good fortune it is
    To partake of a jollification like this ;
And luckier still if the Members encore him,
For he meets at the Steaks, boys, with all that's meet for him.
        Down, down, so well they go down !

The celestial Gridiron is seen overhead,
And below are the worshippers blessedly spread ;
'Tis theirs, in this place, the Iron Age to command,
As 'tis golden to lean on the fat of the land.
        Down, down, it beats the Iron Crown !

Your stupids may prattle o'er soup, fish and fowl,
Of the feast they call reason, the flow they call soul ;
Poor ignorant devils, I grieve for their sakes,
Since their best feasts and flows are but wretched miss steaks.
        Down, down, neither sappy nor brown.

The only real Socialists Europe can boast
Are here, and, without them, the system were lost ;
Jokes, repartees, " tempers," and fleas in the ear,
Are all paid with the ready—there's no Owen here.
      To go down, down, altogether done brown !

I adore the sage Ancient, who stoutly maintains
What is good for the belly is good for the brains.
P's and Q's prigs may practise ; give me the three P's,
And of Port, Punch and Porter, as much as you please.
      To wash down, down, the tender and brown !

He's a delicate monster, your Sir Loin of Beef,
Of succulent food he's the glory and chief ;
But he's cowardly, too, for the fray once begun,
To the last he's inclining to cut and to run.
      Down, down, gravy-ty down.

When the upper side's gone, and the under side's come,
'Tis like Boney's late burial, rather a hum :
Your appetite's cloyed, and you loll on your seat,
And you look on your plate as 'twere *pewtered* meat,
      That will not go down, any how, down.

Yet how pleasant it is from this weary world's toil
To escape and be happy in broil after broil ;
Not a cross to be plagued with, be damned, but endured ;
For if even a cross buttock came 't would be floored.
      Down, down, quickly put down.

Then the Visitors' thanks, with brevity told,
To the glorious Steakers, a century old ;
May they drink, laugh, and love to the end of all time,
And nothing on earth ever Burke the Sublime.
      Derry down, down, up derry down !

Saturday Night, February 6, 1841.—After dining for the fourth time in six weeks with the Sublime : an honour not to be forgotten by the Foundling.

          W. J.

A NEW SONG TO THE TUNE OF YANKEE DOODLE.

By Brother C. W. HALLETT.

YANKEE DOODLE borrows cash,
　　Yankee Doodle spends it ;
　　And then he snaps his fingers at
　　The jolly Flat who lends it.
Ask him when he means to pay,
　　He shews no hesitation,
But says he'll take the shortest way,
　　And that's Repudiation !
　　　　　Chorus, Yankee Doodle, &c.

*Chorus after
all but
the first verse.*

Yankee vows that every state
　　Is free and independent,
And if they paid each other's debts,
　　There'd never be an end on't.
They're quite distinct till Pay-day comes,
　　And then throughout the nation,
They all become " United States "
　　To preach—repudiation !
　　　　　　　Chorus.

Lend your cash to Illinois,
　Or to Massachusett,
Florida, or Mississipi,—
　Ten to one you lose it !
Amongst the States 'tis hard to say
　Which makes the proudest show, sirs,
But Yankees all themselves prefer
　The State of *O-hi-O*, sirs.
Chorus.

The Rev'rend Joker of St. Paul's
　Don't relish much their plunder,
And often at their knavish tricks
　Has hurled his witty thunder.
But Jonathan by nature wears
　A hide of toughest leather,
Which braves the sharpest-pointed darts
　And *canons* put together.
Chorus.

He tells them they are clapping on
　Their credit quite a stopper,
And when they want to go to War,
　They'll never raise a copper.
They only laugh, and coolly say,
　Rather than they'll right us,
They mean to keep our dividends,
　And hoard them up to fight us.
Chorus.

The S. S. B. S.

What's the use of moneyed friends,
  If we must not bleed them?
Ours, I guess, says Jonathan,
  The country is of freedom!
And what does freedom mean, if not
  To whop your slaves at pleasure,
And borrow money when you can,
  To pay it at your leisure?

Chorus.

Great and free Ameriky
  With all the world is vying,
That she's the land of *promise*
  There is surely no denying!
But be it known henceforth to all
  Who hold their I O U, sirs,
A Yankee Doodle's promise is
  A Yankee Doodle *do*, sirs.

Chorus.

THE PARLIAMENT MAN.

By Brother C. W. HALLETT.

IF you think it a gratification
   To work hard without remuneration,
And all for the good of the nation,
      You should serve as a Parliament man.
Look out for some Borough once Rotten,
Which a new independence has gotten,
And that's the most promising spot on
      Which you may carry your plan.
Give out you're the People's best Friend,
Cheap bread and "no Taxes" your end.
            Chorus, If you think it, &c.

In your canvass go bowing and scraping,
While the Rustics around you are gaping,
From the wives there will be no escaping,
      Till some sweet civil things you declare.
You must tell 'em their children are wonders,
And hurl all your bitterest thunders
At the Parliament's short-sighted blunders—
      In not giving votes to the Fair !

They'll vow you're the man of all others,
And secure you their Husbands and Brothers.
                    Chorus.

Then at night you must sup with the Freemen,
Butchers, Bakers, Cheesemongers, and Teamen,
And gobble sufficient for three men,
        Before you can venture to rise.
Swill Warren's Jet Blacking in bumpers,
Make speeches, and tell some huge thumpers,
To catch all the wavering plumpers
        When the day comes to fight for the prize.
Till at last you are wheeled up to bed
Full of *spirits*, but more than half dead.
                    Chorus.

At length comes the day for the polling,
Manœuvres and tricks and cajolling,
Bands of music and banners patrolling,
        All ready for mischief or fun.
On the hustings you take up your station,
Watch anxiously each variation,
Till at last a long loud acclamation,
        Announces the victory won.
The electors you hastily thank,
What a pity you can't write a Frank !
                    Chorus.

Then, no sooner you've taken your seat in
The House, than kind friends are entreating
Your presence at this or that meeting,
 Where Charity's always the plea !
You're invited to move resolutions
For the Polish or Greek Constitutions,
And 'tis hinted that small contributions
 Won't look well from a new made M.P.
Your purse-strings you've daily to draw
For some cause you don't value a straw.
      Chorus.

Then each friend who's been on your committee,
When you canvassed the county or city,
Considers it nothing but fit he
 Should seek some reward for his task.
Your knocker he's daily besetting,
In hopes of immediately getting
Some berth, a good salary netting,—
 A sinecure's all he would ask !
Or his son, who's ambitious to rise,
Would like a small place in th' Excise.
      Chorus.

Then you fag to get up an oration,
Which you think will make quite a sensation,
And procure for your name a bright station
 In the pages of Parliament lore.

With rhetorical flights you have decked it,
And metaphors smart intersect it,
Some are old—but they'll never detect it
　　　In a speech of two columns or more.
In the papers next morning it shines
" Anonymous," squeezed in two lines.
　　　　　　　　　Chorus.

If you're silent, you grow very weary
Of speeches long, heavy, and dreary ;
If you get up yourself they won't hear ye,
　　　And even the Speaker cries " Bar ! "
You may try your wit pungent and Attic,
You may try to be loud and emphatic,
But you'll find all the Members asthmatic,
　　　They're seized with a sudden catarrh :
You grow heartily sick, and would fain
Be at home in the country again.
　　　　　　　　　Chorus.

The occasion you're not long in meeting,
For, by way of your troubles completing,
A petition against you for treating
　　　Is presented to quash your return.
'Tis referred to a chosen Committee,
Who feel for your grievance no pity,
And you sing a most dolorous ditty
　　　When their final decision you learn.
For weeks, to your cost, they're employed ;
In the end, your election is—void.
　　　　　　　　　Chorus.

THE GATES OF SOMNAUTH.

By Brother C. W. HALLETT.

AMONGST the Eastern news I hear
   There's been a mighty shindy,
About a proclamation from
   The Governor of Indy.
Who when he called his army back
   In such a hurry from North,
Desired them to be sure and bring
   Away the gates of Somnauth.
         Oh ! wasn't he a trump to save
           The precious gates of Sandal ?
         To Ellenbro' no other lord
           Is fit to hold a candle.

Eight hundred years ago, or more,
   The Sultan whopped the Hindoos,
And battered all their Temples down,
   And prigged the doors and windows.
Amongst the plunder which he got,
   These gates were then included,
And ever since, the story goes,
   They've o'er the insult brooded.
                Chorus.

The S. S. B. S.

So, after all these centuries,
  The foul disgrace to wipe out,
Brave General Nott was ordered off
  To put the Sultan's pipe out.
He sat him down before Ghuznee,
  Not in a very calm mood,
And swore he'd have the gates away
  Which guard the Tomb of Mahmoud.
                  Chorus.

He bore the prize in triumph off
  Like Samson, on his shoulders,
To strike with awe, of British power,
  The hearts of all beholders.
As if through India could be found
  A dozen witless mortals,
Who cared one single damn about
  A pair of rusty Portals.
                  Chorus.

And when at last, the trophies rare,
  Had reached their destination,
And all the troops were ordered out
  To hail their restoration,
The Native Princes, mighty Chiefs,
  And all the Petty States, too,
The deuce of any Temple was
  There left to hang the gates to.
                  Chorus.

Some said he meant to build the Temple
  Up again, and *buy* dolls,
And set them up within the gates
  To go and worship *Idols.*
The Duke, good pious man, repelled
  This base insinuation,
And as to Idols, voted it
  An Idle accusation.
                Chorus.

When first he sought these mouldy gates,
  And raked them with their rust up,
He little thought in England he
  Was kicking such a dust up.
Such wondrous changes in the world
  He never could foresee, then,
As Whigs, Defenders of the Faith,
  And Tories, all but Heathen.
                Chorus.

But when the noble lord was baulked
  In all his Eastern glory,
And homeward bound, his chalks he walked,
  . His raven locks turned hoary.
Altho' he took a final leave
  Of all the copper dingies,
The Cockneys say these gates would long
  Remind him of the *Hinges.*
                Chorus.

THE FRENCH REVOLUTION, 1848.

By Brother C. W. HALLETT.

’TIS a very fine thing to pull down a King
And set up a new Constitution;
To kick up a row, never mind when or how,
For the sake of a grand revolution.
Huzza for the French Revolution !
Success to the New Constitution !
’Tis a very fine thing to pull down a king.
And get up a grand revolution !
Chorus, Huzza, &c.

How long did we praise the glorious three days
Of the famous July revolution,
When Parisian blades and stout barricades
Accomplished the grand revolution ?
When Louis Philippe’s elocution
Assured them a new constitution,
“ Vive le Roi,” did they sing to the Citizen King,
The King of the grand revolution.
Chorus.

But only just wait till the year Forty-eight,
   And another sublime revolution
Knocks everything down, and snatches the Crown
   From the King of the grand revolution.
Then hey, for the grand revolution,
   And then for the grand distribution
Of the loaves and the fishes, which everyone wishes,
   Who helps in a grand revolution.
                              Chorus.

Some half-dozen meet at the end of a street,
   With smiling and confident faces,
And those modest-elves, coolly helping themselves,
   Volunteer for the ministers' places :
Thus cunningly filling the parts up,
   The " Provisional Government " starts up,
And they issue decrees, as busy as bees,
   While the shouts of the mob keep their hearts up.
                              Chorus.

One takes the Marine, while another is seen
   For " War and the Army" providing ;
A third " Public Works," and nobody shirks
   O'er " Justice" and " Commerce " presiding.
But the boldest of all men in France is,
   The man who against all the chances
Of a treasury low and credit " no go,"
   Can tackle their rotten finances.
                              Chorus.

They promise a deal for the National weal,—
    And the poor public purse, how they sweat it ;
Less work and more pay, is the cant of the day,
    And the people all "wish they may get it."
They don't recollect that their masters,
    For fear of still further disasters,
May all cut away, and leave them some day
    Without either wages or masters.
                       Chorus.

Poor Louis Philippe, tho' thought pretty deep,
    By the sudden attack was confounded ;
He called for Nemours to turn out of doors
    The mob who his person surrounded :
But he found that the game was all over,—
    No more could he lodge there in clover,
But must e'en cut his stick, and be off pretty quick,
    By the packet to Brighton or Dover.
                       Chorus.

So he packed up his bag, tho' he scarce had a rag,
    And his pocket contained not a Stiver ;
He sent for a cab, and had just time to grab
    Three francs and a half for the driver.
He made for the coast in a hurry,
    And there he embarked in a flurry ;
With his whiskers all shaven, he steered for Newhaven,
    To take his abode up in Surrey.
                       Chorus.

Now landed once more on Albion's shore—
   The refuge of all persecution—
   Securely may he in the land of the free
Learn to value a free constitution :
   And may we, with combined resolution,
Preserve our beloved Constitution ;
   Nor e'er with rash haste, be ambitious to taste
The sweets of a French Revolution.

Chorus.
A fig for the French Revolution,
   We want not a new Constitution,
   But will always be seen in defence of the Queen,
   And we won't have a French Revolution.

THE MARVELLOUS TONGUE.

By Brother C. W. HALLETT.

YOU all, no doubt, have heard me talk
   Of a wonderful leg that was made of cork,
But now of a much more marvellous thing
Than an L. E. G. I am going to sing.
      Ri tooral looral lodity to
      Ri tooral looral la.

One Jonathan Glib had a scolding wife,
Whose termagant tongue was the pest of his life ;
He consulted a conjuror how to allay her,
But she couldn't be *soothed* even by a *soothsayer*.
                    Chorus.

Says the sage, "Your misfortune must be endured,
For a scolding wife can never be cured ;
But if you're inclined her steps to follow,
I'll give you a tongue that shall beat hers hollow."
                    Chorus.

This plan succeeded remarkably well ;
The man got a *Clapper* that silenced his *belle;*
But soon, to his cost, the unfortunate elf
Found out that he never could silence himself.
Chorus.

His tongue of a subject ne'er found any lack,
For all about nothing for hours 'twould clack ;
It was just like a river whose banks couldn't prop it,
For though you might *dam* it, you never could stop it.
Chorus.

All alone in the stage once he made such a din,
That coachee, without ever looking within,
Refused all the passers that wanted to ride,
For he thought from the noise he had six inside.
Chorus.

He was next taken up for some little *faux pas*,
And he chattered so fast when placed at the bar,
That the Justice exclaimed, " Hold your tongue, rude man."
Says he, " You may hold it yourself, if you can."
Chorus.

Talking to him was both meat and drink ;
Of his latter end he'd no time to think ;
But he wore out his lungs, and he grew so ill
That he died—but his tongue kept wagging on still.
Chorus.

His friends attended his grave in a throng,
In hopes that death had silenced his tongue ;
But he swore, as mutes were attending for pelf,
He'd be d——d if he'd be a mute himself.
Chorus.

He talked to the Sexton—he talked to the Clerk—
He talked to the Mourners as gay as a lark ;
And the Parson, by whom he should be interred,
Gave it up, for he couldn't get in a word.
Chorus.

In the midst of his story, as nothing would stop him,
Snug under the turf they managed to pop him ;
But tho' on his head they piled a mound,
He went on with his tale when under ground.
Chorus.

How long he talked, 'tis hard to say ;
But the grave was opened the other day,
And the skull was all that remained of the dead,
But the teeth were chattering still in the head.
Chorus.

The people in crowds this sight did bring :
And, what is a most miraculous thing,
Whoever once held that skull in his paw,
Could never afterwards *hold his jaw*.
Chorus.

THE STEAM NAG.

By Brother C. W. HALLETT.

SAM CROTCHET while sitting at breakfast one day,
    In his snug little parlour, was thus heard to say,
When the kettle was hissing and puffing out steam,—
" Ods bobs, I've just thought of a capital scheme !"
                        Gee ho, Dobbin, &c.

In these days of steam-coaches and boats and what not,
All may travel who understand boiling the pot ;
And since of equestrian skill I can brag,
I'll try if I can't contrive a steam nag.
                        Gee ho, Dobbin, &c.

No longer I'll sit in the dismals at home,
But in search of adventures and science I'll roam :
I'm sick of reviews, magazines, and newspapers,
I'll ride out by steam to get rid of the vapours.
                        Gee ho, Dobbin, &c.

Then his kettle he clapped on a pan of hot coal,
With a saddle and housings surmounting the whole ;
No *stirrups* he wanted to perfect his trim,
But a poke of the fire was a *stir-up* for him.

> Gee ho, Dobbin, &c.

He mounted his nag, and went off like a shot
As soon as the reins in his fingers he got ;
He looked very fierce when astride on his kettle,
And none could deny he'd a horse of real *metal*.

> Gee ho, Dobbin, &c.

He galloped through high-roads and bye-roads and lanes,
And the kettle poured forth most melodious strains,
Whose music it sang is a point of some doubt,
But it couldn't be Handel's, it came from the spout.

> Gee ho, Dobbin, &c.

He went out with the hounds, of sport a true lover,
And stuck to the *lid*, as he jogged to the *cover;*
To be in at the death, too he made a great rush,
Lest his flue should want sweeping he'd fain get the brush.

> Gee ho, Dobbin, &c.

Over hedges and ditches he flew at full speed,
For nothing could stop his impetuous steed ;
And though as a horseman none ever was bolder,
Sam found that he wasn't a good kettleholder.

> Gee ho, Dobbin, &c.

Till night over heath, fen, and brier he jogged,
When all of a sudden he found himself bogged ;
He whipped and he spurred to get out of the clay,
But his hobby ran restive and gave him a "*nay*."

                              Gee ho, Dobbin, &c.

Balaam's ass, we are told, once stopped short in the road,
And lectured his master his back who bestrode ;
But Sam got that night from his fiery hack
A blow up, that laid him quite flat on his back.

                              Gee ho, Dobbin, &c.

The boiler it flew into millions of bits,
And poor Sammy Crotchet was kicked into fits ;
He was dashed to the ground, and he thought as he struck it,
As the boiler kicked him he must needs kick the bucket.

                              Gee ho, Dobbin, &c.

The bubble as well as the boiler was burst,
But still would his head run on steam as at first ;
So to humour his fancy he married a wife,
And lived in hot water the rest of his life.

                              Gee ho, Dobbin, &c.

THE PEACE CONGRESS OF 1849.

By Brother C. W. HALLETT.

MR. POPS was a quiet man,
    Heigho, fiddle-de-dee ;
He heard with joy of the novel plan.
For a general peace, and off he ran,
    To put down his name, did he.
        To put down his name, did he.

He went to a meeting, and there they passed,
    Heigho, fiddle-de-dee ;
A resolution that wars should cease,
And all the world be for ever at peace
    And live in harmony.
        And live in harmony.

And so to accomplish this wonderful change,
    Heigho, fiddle-de-dee ;
They all engaged their help to lend,
And promised, if needful, their money to spend
    For such a felicity.
        For such a felicity.

They first shook hands with the peace-loving French,
    Heigho, fiddle-de-dee ;
Who were battering down the walls of Rome,
And daily increasing their army at home,
    But all in amity.
        But all in amity.

They supported the brave Hungarian cause,
    Heigho, fiddle-de-dee ;
They were sorry they couldn't go out to fight,
But they wished 'em success with all their might,
    And gave them their sympathy.
        And gave them their sympathy.

They admired the moral force Repealers,
    Heigho, fiddle-de-dee ;
For it sounded well, though at Limerick
It ended in showers of stones and brick,
    And a pretty severe shindy.
        And a pretty severe shindy.

And now they're full of lamentations,
    Heigho, fiddle-de-dee ;
That we don't more tender mercy show
To the innocent pirates of Borneo,
    And the Dyack family.
        And the Dyack family.

The S. S. B. S.

Instead of attending with fire and sword,
    Heigho, fiddle-de-dee ;
We should salt their tails, and invite them all
To a six hours' lecture at Exeter Hall
    On the sin of piracy.
        On the sin of piracy.

They'll send out next to the Caffre tribes,
    Heigho, fiddle-de-dee ;
And urge them to give up agitation,
And submit all their claims to arbitration,
    Whenever they can't agree.
        Whenever they can't agree.

And as to the wild and turbulent Sikhs,
    Heigho, fiddle-de-dee ;
When we're all disarmed they'll be far too moral
To think of seeking another quarrel,
    And peaceable subjects be.
        And peaceable subjects be.

All laws, of course, must be abolished,
    Heigho, fiddle-de-dee ;
There's to be an end of litigation,
And all be done by consultation,
    Without reward or fee.
        Without reward or fee.

But what's to become of the hands turn'd loose?
 Heigho, fiddle-de-dee ;
The soldiers and sailors, with lawyers to back 'em,
Will get up a war of their own, and whack 'em,
 From sheer necessity.
  From sheer necessity.

In short, they'll find, or I'm much mistaken,
 Heigho, fiddle-de-dee ;
That to make all the world embrace one another,
And every foe become a brother,
 Will end in fiddle-de-dee.
  Will end in fiddle-de-dee.

RAPHAEL AND O'CONNELL.

By Brother C. W. HALLETT.

SAYS Raphael to O'Connell Dan,
    " They tell me you're the very man
That, if you will, most surely can
    Procure me a seat in the Commons.
For I have wanted long to see
My name embellished with M.P.,
And thought how pleasant it would be
To get by post my letters free ;
But Westminster would not be had,
And Pomfret, too, I found as bad,
And Evesham said I warn't the lad
    To send to a seat in the Commons."

Chorus.

Hocus, pocus, winkey fum,
Robbery, jobbery, gammon and hum,
Oh ! isn't Dan a subject rum
To deal for a seat in the Commons.

" Oh ! then," says Dan, "leave all to me,
And soon I'll fit you to a T,
If you'll fork out a decent fee
    To pay for your seat in the Commons.

There's Carlow wants a candidate,
And I'll go bail you shan't be bate,
So now's the time to try your fate,
If you don't cry 'done,' you'll be too late.
You've only just to write a cheque,
You'll never meet with a safer spec.,
Two thousand pounds is all the pec.
    I ask for your seat in the Commons.

Chorus.

" Sit down and pen a bold address,
And mind you lay a handsome stress
On Ireland's wrongs, and vow redress
    When you get your seat in the Commons.
Or if to write you've ne'er been taught,
Or a letter costs too much of thought,
Just hand me out the one you bought
When Westminster was to be fought ;
I'll dress it up with phrases new,
And throw a patriotic hue
O'er everything you say or do,
    To secure your seat in the Commons."

Chorus.

Dan wrote that night himself direct,
And bade the Carlow Boys reject
All other comers, to elect
    His friend to a seat in the Commons.

Says he, " I have been told, 'tis true,
My friend is but a dirty screw,
And that his word's not worth a sous ;
But what is that to me or you?
It's all a pack of stuff,—why, zounds !
He's going to pay two thousand pounds,
I should like to know what better grounds
    There can be for a seat in the Commons."
                Chorus.

Next time they met, " My boy," says Dan,
" I tould you you should be the man,
If you would but embrace my plan
    To secure your seat in the Commons.
'Tis just as I prognosticated,—
Already you've been nominated,
And that with us is estimated
Just as good as being sated.
Success will soon your efforts crown,
The Orange Boys we've quite done brown,
So——just pay half the money down,
    To secure your seat in the Commons."
                Chorus.

His visit soon did Dan repeat,
And with a smile the ex-sheriff greet.
Says he, " Your joy is now complete,
    You may take your seat in the Commons.

The victory's won—you're dubbed M.P.,
And now may send your letters free ;
So cry Huzza ! for liber*ty*,
And——tip the balance due to me.
What makes you thus your shoulders shrug,
And twist about your ugly mug?
You're just as snug as a bug in a rug
    When you take your seat in the Commons."
                    Chorus.

But soon petitions two or three
Against him did the Member see,
And Dan was called for—guarantee,
    To defend his seat in the Commons.
" Oh, no !" says Dan, " I'm up to snuff,
One contest, sure, is quantum suff. ;
You've been elected, that's enough,—
You've had the honour, I the stuff.
I tould you we should surely beat,
And so we will, if you're discreet ;
I mean, we'll beat—a quick retreat,
    And give up your seat in the Commons."
                    Chorus.

THE PENNY POSTAGE.

By Brother C. W. HALLETT.

A BUMPER let's fill to the great Rowland Hill,
   The wisest of all modern sages ;
The finger of Fame will point to his name
   As it figures in History's pages.
In War 'tis renowned wherever 'tis found,
   In the Pulpit it shines above many ;
And now with fresh laurels it ought to be crown'd—
   Since our letters all go for a penny.
        Chorus, A bumper let's fill, &c.

Our Treasury's low, and our credit so-so ;
   Of our cash we're obliged to be sparing ;
And how we shall make both ends meet I don't know—
   'Tis a subject that's getting past *Baring*.
New taxes, they say, we shall soon have to pay,
   In spite of Joe Hume, from Kilkenny ;
But whatever the Budget, we never need grudge it—
   Our letters all go for a penny.
        Chorus.

Of many wise saws about freedom and laws
  We prate, with our arms stuck a-kimbo,
Tho' the Sheriffs of London, in Liberty's cause,
  Are clapped by the Commons in limbo.
Each Tory and Whig about freedom talks big ;
  But, if others would have it, why then he
Soon alters his tone ; but we don't care a fig—
  Since our letters all go for a penny.
                                    Chorus.

The Church is in dread of being knocked on the head,
  And of sooner or later being undone ;
And some even hope that his Rev'rence, the Pope,
  Will appoint the next Bishop of London.
As for me, I don't care under what saint we are,
  St. Patrick, St. George, or St. Denis,
To me 'tis all one if we've any or none—
  Since our letters all go for a penny.
                                    Chorus.

The Chartists in arms have been spreading alarms
  'Mongst the good country folks and their spouses ;
The farmers don't think themselves safe in their farms,
  Nor the gentlemen safe in their houses.
Through England and Wales the commotion prevails,
  From Berwick to Abergavenny ;
But no matter how rife are rebellion and strife—
  Since our letters all go for a penny.
                                    Chorus.

What efforts are made to put down the Slave Trade,
   And the shackles of freedom to sever !
But nothing will do, and King Dingy-Tattoo
   Sells his subjects as freely as ever.
All the money we pay is so much thrown away,
   We've been mighty big fools to give any.
But I care not a rush how much freedom we crush—
   Since our letters all go for a penny.
                     Chorus.

Our old wooden walls, which have weathered tough squalls,
   And have long been an Englishman's glory,
Are left to get rotten and almost forgotten,
   Except in the pages of story.
There's a mighty to-do that our ships are too few,
   And the Russians and French are too many ;
But a fig for the Navy ! I don't care a sous—
   Since our letters all go for a penny.
                     Chorus.

There are rumours of war breaking out from afar—
   East and west there are signs of commotion ;
The Russians are scheming, the Yankees are dreaming
   Of vict'ry for once on the Ocean.
In short, we're, I guess, in a bit of a mess :
   But who would e'er be such a ninny
As to trouble his pate about matters of State—
   Since our letters all go for a penny.
                     Chorus.

OLD CLO'.

By Brother C. W. HALLETT.

AS I was a sitting in the Parliament House,
    In the gallery corner, as still as a mouse—
Chisholm Anstey was talking—I began to snore,
When there came all at once a loud knock at the door.
(*Knock.*)   Who's dat knocking at de door?
          Who's dat knocking at de door?
          Is dat Old Joe?
          No, it am Old Clo'.
Well, he can't come in, so he'd better go,
    For it's no use knocking at de door
          Any more,
It's no use knocking at de door.

He's just been elected a new M.P.
For the City of London, the great and the free,
And he's come down at once, in a deuce of a heat,
Just to try it on boldly, and claim his seat.
(*Knock.*)   Who's dat knocking at de door, &c.,
          Is dat Old Clo'?
          Yes, it am, by Jo!
Well, he's not good-looking, and he can't come in,
    For it's no use knocking at de door, &c.

Tell him, says the Speaker, we can't let him in,
So it's no use his making such a devil of a din ;
We've a big oath to swallow that he'll find rather queer,
And, if he doesn't gulp it, he can't lodge here.
(*Knock.*)   Who's dat knocking at de door? &c.,
         Is dat our Ben ?
         No, it's Old Clo' again.
   Well, he's got a hook nose, and he can't come in,
      So it's no use knocking at de door, &c.

He says the City sent him with unanimous voice,
And they won't be chiselled out of the man of their choice ;
So, if you shut him out, there'll be a rare to-do
With the Lord Mayor, and Aldermen, and Common Council, too.
(*Knock.*)   Who's dat knocking at de door? &c.,
         Is dat Mr. Muntz?
         No, it's Old Clo' for once.
   Well, he's got a long beard, and he can't come in,
      So it's no use knocking at de door, &c.

Till we have been to the Lords for advice,
And they won't let us have a Jew at any price,
So just bid the Citizens not to make a pother,
But take back their Member and send us another.
(*Knock.*)   Who's dat knocking at de door? &c.,
         Is dat Friend Bright ?
         No, it's Old Clo' in sight !
   Well, though he looks demure, he can't come in,
      So it's no use knocking at de door, &c.

He's come back to say that the bold City men
Have had a new election and sent him again ;
So you can't shake him off with all your might,
And he'll stay here knocking at de door all night.
(*Knock*.)   Who's dat knocking at de door? &c.,
          What ! Old Clo' again ?
          Yes, Old Clo' again.
    [*Well, tell him, (spoken*).]   Just to wait till next Session,
          and p'rhaps we'll let him in.
       But it's no use knocking at de door
                 Any more,
       It's no use knocking at the door.

AN HISTORICAL STORY.

By WILLIAM BOLLAND, Esq.

AIR, "George Barnwell."

I 'LL tell you all an historical story
   Not very short and not very long,
And if you think that it won't bore ye,
   I'll try and put it into song.

AIR, "Isle of Beauty."

Rufus, when our shores invading,
   Landed at Hungerford Stairs.
But was caught in Windsor Forest
   Shortly after, snaring hares.

AIR, "Barcarolle in Massaniello."

So of his throne he was deprived,
   The sceptre came to Mary's hand,
She for a husband advertised,
   Three persons applied, as I understand

And first the Conqueror came : said he,
  I'll make you my bride.
But William the Third so pressed his plea
  She could not decide
Till Cromwell came to settle this nice affair ;
  He haltered the Queen and sold her at Bartlemy Fair.

AIR, "What equals on Earth."—*Freischütz.*

Just then a young man
  Who was christened Napoleon,
And bore over his brow the bright olive of peace,
  Put in his claim for the throne of Old England,
And bought a new crown upon Mary's decease.

AIR, "Meet me by Moonlight alone."

But Nelson met him one day
  On the Plain of the famed Flodden Field ;
They fought till the Persian array
  On a neighbouring hill made them yield.

So the crown came to Harry the Eighth.
So the crown came to Harry the Eighth.

AIR, "Believe me, if all those endearing young charms."

Who believing 'twas madness in kings to take wife
  Resolved, with an oath, to live free,
And tho' six or seven young women bother'd his life
  Unmarried and single liv'd he.

The S. S. B. S.

It cannot be true, but at least it was said
  That he jilted poor Elizabeth.
And the story so bothered his innocent head
  As to end in his premature death.

AIR, "Oh, Pilot, 'tis a fearful night."

But Stephen he, at fearful risk,
  Fought Richard for his right ;
And freely shed at Bannockburn
  Their royal blood in fight.
Then Stephen, by a cannon-ball,
  Got Richard in his power,
And famed Wat Tyler smothered him
  In onions in the Tower.

AIR, "The Dogs' Meat Man."

But Anne, the old maid, crooked Richard's coz,
  To avenge his cause resolved was.
She got Mr. Brougham to plead her case,
  And Stephen was stoned, up in Waterloo Place.
But she was not long to enjoy her bliss,
  For John came down : upon seeing this
He gave her the choice, 'twixt the dagger or the drink,
  Says she, I'll have the lush, I rather think.

AIR, " A Fine Old English Gentleman."

But as our glorious country boasts
　　A long and ancient line,
And as some other folks here sing
　　Far better songs than mine,

AIR, " We Have Lived and Loved Together."

Let generosity to-night on every brow be seen,
　　And join in loyal harmony
To bless our gracious Queen.
　　God save our gracious Queen, &c., &c.

This song was not written expressly for the S. S. B. S.　It was written by a son of Brother Bolland, and given by him to Brother Fredk. Ponsonby, who has so identified it with the Society that it will not probably be considered out of place in these pages.

ANTHEM,

ON THE OPENING OF THE NEW BEEF-STEAK ROOMS IN THE
PRESENT LYCEUM THEATRE, NOVEMBER, 1838.

By Brother C. W. HALLETT.

ONCE more 'neath a roof of our own are we housed,
    On the very same spot where so oft we've caroused,
Where Apollo and Bacchus the cause have espoused
    Of the jolly old Steakers of England !
    Oh ! the old English Beefsteaks !

O'er our heads the old Gridiron spreading its rays,
The sun of our table, whose glorious blaze
Warms to life the chilled memory of past happy days
    With the jolly old Steakers of England, &c.

What a host of bright names to our memories dear,
In its magical circle in fancy appear,
Crowding round the old Bars which once furnished their cheer,
    To the jolly old Steakers of England, &c.

First *Rich*, who this feast of the Gridiron planned,
And formed with a touch of his Harlequin's wand,
Out of mighty rude matter this Brotherly Band :
    The jolly old Steakers of England, &c.

Then *Hogarth* was a Steaker devoted and true,
For in France, when the gate of proud Calais he drew,
A good English Sirloin he placed full in view,
    Singing, Oh ! the roast beef of old England, &c.

And *Garrick*, the wonder and boast of his age,
The Pet of the Muses, the pride of the stage,
How he loved in the struggle of wit to engage
    With the jolly old Steakers of England, &c.

John *Wilkes*, to whom Liberty's name was so dear
That in search of the Gem he spent half his career,
If elsewhere disappointed, at least found it here,
    With the jolly old Steakers of England, &c.

And *Norfolk's* great Duke, who belonged to the breed
Of the sturdy old Barons of famed Runnymede,
In the same cause of freedom delighted to feed
    With the jolly old Steakers of England, &c.

With loud mimic fury John *Kemble* would foam
In defence of the freedom of Greece or of Rome,
But the freedom of real life he loved best at home,
    With the jolly old Steakers of England, &c.

First *George*, Prince of Wales, and then York's royal Duke,
For the wit of this Board other pleasures forsook,
And of Port wine and Punch they both freely partook
    With the jolly old Steakers of England, &c.

The S. S. B. S.

William *Linley*, the gentle, the simple, the kind,
Whose soft-flowing music reflected his mind,
Like Orpheus, could charm even *brutes*, when he dined
    With the jolly old Steakers of England, &c.

John *Richards* a niche in our history claims,
Tho' he now wastes his prattle on Datchet's fair Dames,
And prefers the dull twaddle of old Father Thames,
    To the jolly old Steakers of England, &c.

Charles *Morris*, our Bard, we have next to record,
Of the Muses at once both the Slave and the Lord ;
In life how applauded, in death how deplored,
    By the jolly old Steakers of England, &c.

James *Lonsdale* we miss, too, as one of the great,
In bulk as in talent—in wit as in weight—
How he gladdened the heart while he painted the pate
   . Of the jolly old Steakers of England, &c.

Lord Chancellor *Brougham* is now pensioned in clover,
He spends all his time between Calais and Dover,
And thinks with regret, when he gets half-seas over,
    Of the jolly old Steakers of England, &c.

Death has snatched our brave Admiral *Dundas* off the list,
Whose pluck could all other foes stoutly resist,
Braver Sailor ne'er stepped, warmer friend was ne'er missed,
    By the jolly old Steakers of England, &c.

Poor *Ferguson's* gone, too, our corporal bold,
Whose heart was cut out in the true British mould ;
Ne'er, till death, did that heart for a moment grow cold
    To the jolly old Steakers of England, &c.

A sigh of regret let us breathe o'er the bier
Of the last royal Duke * who once loved our good cheer,
Forgetting the Prince in the Brother when here,
    With the jolly old Steakers of England, &c.

Sam *Arnold* we mourn, whose melodious voice
Sweetly warbled the favourite airs of our choice ;
No more shall his rich thrilling notes e'er rejoice
    The jolly old Steakers of England, &c.

To *Saltoun* all honour as Chieftain and Lord,
But more for the deeds of his unsullied sword ;
Of Waterloo's Heroes, what name more adored
    Than that jolly old Steaker of England? &c.

Our *Stephenson's* gone, whose bright fancy gave birth
To shrewd maxims of wit, set in flashes of mirth,
The last of the giants that lingered on earth
    Mid the jolly old Steakers of England, &c. †

Lastly *Hallett*, our time-honoured Poet, who long
Charmed us all with his worth and the wit of his song,
And bequeathed these rich gems of his genius among
    The jolly old Steakers of England, &c.†

* H.R.H. the Duke of Sussex.
† These verses were added after Brother Hallett's death.

With the mem'ry of genius so bright in the sire,
Let each son try to catch but one spark of that fire
Which the Gridiron's classic remains should inspire
    In the jolly old Steakers of England, &c.

May that relic survive, as with care it needs must,
Till the last of its votaries is laid in the dust,
And then, let it mingle its time-honoured rust,
    With the jolly old Steakers of England, &c.

CATALOGUE OF EFFECTS

THE PROPERTY OF THE

SUBLIME SOCIETY OF BEEF STEAKS,

SOLD AT

Messrs. CHRISTIE, MANSON, & WOODS',

On WEDNESDAY, APRIL 7, 1869.

ENGRAVED PORTRAITS OF THE MEMBERS, &c.,

GLAZED, IN OAK FRAMES, WITH THE GRIDIRON IN METAL.

Lot		£	s.	d.
1	Rich, the Founder, as Harlequin	2	4	0
2	The Stage's Glory—a frontispiece	1	13	0
3	The Beggar's Opera, after Hogarth, by Blake	2	0	0
4	J. Cobb	0	11	0
5	Thos. Tickle, after Thurston, by Finden	1	1	0
6	Paul Whitehead, after Gainsborough, by Collier	0	13	0
7	Gabriel Hunt, after Hogarth, by Livesay	2	0	0
8	J. Fergusson, of Pitfour	0	13	0
9	Hogarth before his easel	2	14	0
10	Aaron Hill, by Hulsbergh	1	9	0
11	Rob. Baldey, after B. Wilson, by Fisher	0	17	0
12	J. Wilkes, after Pine, by Sibelius	2	2	0
13	D. Garrick, after Pine, by Dickinson	2	4	0
14	C. Churchill, after Schaah, by Burford	0	17	0
15	Isaac Ware, from a bust, by Roubillac	0	14	0
16	Antony Askew, M. D.	1	1	0
17	A. Murphy, after Dance, by Ward	2	2	0
	Carried forward	24	15	0

LOT		£	s.	d.
	Brought forward	24	15	0
18	J. Mingay, after Romney, by Hodges . . .	0	16	0
19	R. Grindall—mezzotint	0	15	0
20	Beard, after Hudson, by McArdell . . .	1	0	0
21	J. Bradshaw, after H. Morland, by Smith . .	1	1	0
22	G. Lambert, after Vanderbank, by Faber . .	2	0	0
23	R. Glover	0	19	0
24	J. P. Kemble, after Shee, by Sharp . . .	1	12	0
25	The Marquis Thomond, after the Marchioness of Thomond,			
	by Meadows	0	13	0
26	G. Colman, after Sir J. Reynolds, by Scriven . .	1	2	0
27	Sir John Cam Hobhouse, after Lonsdale, by Turner .	0	13	0
28	Sir H. Englefield, after Phillips, by ditto . .	0	13	0
29	The Earl of Sandwich, after Gainsborough, by Sherwin	0	15	0
30	T. King, after Dance, by Daniell . . .	0	15	0
31	George IV., when Prince of Wales, after De Roscer, by			
	Reynolds	1	1	0
32	The Duke of York, after Beechey, by Skelton .	1	2	0
33	The Duke of Sussex, after ditto, by ditto . .	3	5	0
34	The Lord Mayor (M. Wood), after Devis, by Jay .	0	15	0
35	Sir F. Burdett, after Northcote, by Sharp . .	1	10	0
36	The Earl of Suffolk, after Oliver, by Bragg . .	1	10	0
37	Lord Brougham, after Lonsdale, by Lupton . .	1	10	0
38	Admiral Dundas, after ditto, by Cousins . .	0	16	0
39	James Lonsdale, by Turner	1	1	0
40	Baron Heath, after Lonsdale, by Cousins . .	0	14	0
41	W. Linley, after ditto, by Sherlock . . .	0	13	0
42	R. Liston, after Grant, by Bromley . . .	1	3	0
43	Sir R. C. Ferguson, after Smith, by Lupton . .	2	12	0
44	The Hon. Fox Maule, after Duncan, by Porter . .	8	0	0
45	The Duke of Leinster, after Smith, by Saunders .	2	2	0
46	Lord Saltoun, lithograph, after Baugniet . .	2	2	0
47	Rowland Alston, ditto	1	18	0
	Carried forward	69	3	0

DRAWINGS,

GLAZED, IN OAK FRAMES, WITH THE GRIDIRON IN METAL.

G. P. HARDING.

LOT		£	s.	d.
	Brought forward	69	3	0
48	Thomas Hudson, artist, and master of Sir J. Reynolds, pencil drawing after a portrait by his father-in-law Richardson .	3	5	0

W. HAINES.

49	C. W. Hallett—*water colours*	2	5	0
50	The Earl of Guilford—*pencil*	2	4	0

TH. BRIDYFORD, A.R.H.A.

51	Judge Bolland—*pencil*	2	6	0

J. LONSDALE.

52	Th. Lewin—*chalks*	3	0	0

DEIGHTON.

53	Sir A. Barnard	3	3	0

G. P. HARDING.

54	J. Hippisley, comedian—*pencil*	1	18	0

G. P. HARDING.

55	W. Nettleship, after Joseph—*pencil* . . .	3	8	0
	Carried forward	90	12	0

PORTRAITS IN OIL BY J. LONSDALE.

Lot		£	s.	d.
	Brought forward	90	12	0
56	H.R.H. The Duke of Sussex	5	15	6
57	The Duke of Argyll—*unframed*	4	15	0
58	The Knight of Kerry	8	0	0
59	Dr. Somerville	8	0	0
60	Charles Morris	8	10	0
61	John Richards, the Recorder of the Society . .	5	5	0
62	Lord Broughton	7	5	0
63	James Lonsdale, by R. F. Lonsdale	1	5	0
64	E. T. Lonsdale, copied by his brother from a picture by his father	1	5	0

SILVER—at per oz.

		£	s.	d.
65	Six forks, threaded fiddle-pattern, with the gridiron and arms, and crests of members	5	18	10
66	Ten ditto	8	11	2
67	Six ditto—*not engraved*	4	13	0
68	Six table-spoons, with the gridiron and inscriptions . .	4	12	0
69	Six ditto, with the gridiron	4	8	8
70	Six salt-spoons	1	3	2
71	Four mustard-spoons	1	6	2
72	A sugar-ladle	1	1	0
73	A punch-ladle, with fluted silver bowl, and horn handle, inscribed " Ex dono Barington Bradshaw " . .	3	5	0
74	A Fine Ditto, with leaf-shaped bowl, the handle terminating in a gridiron, inlaid with a Queen Anne guinea. *Dated* 1735	14	5	0
	Carried forward	189	16	6

LOT		£	s.	d.
	Brought forward	189	16.	6
75	The ribbon and badge of the president, formed as a silver gridiron. *Dated* 1735	23	2	6
76	An oblong cheese-toaster, with gadrooned edge . .	12	6	0
76A	A Wine Funnel	1	7	3
77	A FINE COUTEAU DE CHASSE, with engraved and pierced blade, the handle formed of a group of Mars, Venus, and Cupid in silver, the mounting of the sheath of openwork silver, chased with arabesque figures, scrolls and flowers. *The reputed work of B. Cellini*—inscribed " Ex Dono Antonio Askew, M. D."	84	0	0
78	A brown stoneware jug, with silver lid and mounting—the thumbpiece formed as a gridiron	7	0	0
79	A ditto	6	6	0

MISCELLANEOUS.

80	An oval ivory snuff-box, with a cameo of Dante on the lid and inscription inside. " Presented to the S.S.B.S. by B. G. B. (Dr. Babington), an honorary member. The cameo of Dante on the lid of this box was carved by its donor, and its wood formed part of a mummy-case brought by him from Egypt in 1815 ; the surrounding ivory was turned by a friend "—*in a leather case*	10	0	0
81	A circular snuff-box, formed of oak dug from the ruins of the old Lyceum Theatre after its destruction by fire ; a silver shield engraved with the gridiron on the lid . .	4	0	0
82	A wooden punch-ladle, with openwork handle, and ten doyleys	1	6	0
83	A cigar-case, formed of a curious piece of oak . . .	2	0	0
84	A pair of halberds	3	10	0
	Carried forward	344	14	3

Lot		£	s.	d.
	Brought forward	344	14	3
85	A large Oriental punch-bowl, enamelled with figures, butter-flies, and flowers, inside and out—in a case. *Presented by the late Lord Saltoun, K.G.*	17	15	0
86	Another, enamelled with figures and baskets of flowers in medallions, with red and gold scale borders. *Presented by Baron Heath*	9	5	0
87	A ditto, enamelled with figures	2	4	0
88	A fluted ditto, with flowers	1	10	0
89	The President's hat, a hat said to have belonged to Garrick, and a cardinal's hat	0	15	0
90	" The Mitre of the late Cardinal Gregorio, offered to the Sublime Society of the Beef Steaks by Brother W. Somer-ville "—*in silk case.*	0	13	0
91	Facsimile of an agreement between Rich and C. Fleet-wood—*framed and glazed*	0	10	0
92	BUST OF JOHN WILKES—*in marble* . . .	23	2	0
	Carried forward	400	8	3

GLASS, &c.,

ENGRAVED WITH THE GRIDIRON AND MOTTO.

LOT		£	s.	d.
	Brought forward	400	8	3
93	A pair of wine-glasses			
94	A pair of ditto			
95	A pair of ditto			
96	A pair of ditto			
97	A pair of ditto			
98	A pair of ditto			
99	A pair of ditto			
100	A pair of ditto			
101	A pair of ditto			
102	Four decanters	45	1	0
102 A	Two decanters			
103	Six large pewter dishes			
104	Four smaller ditto			
105	Twelve plates			
106	Twelve plates			
107	Thirteen ditto			
108	Twelve hot-water ditto			
109	Twelve ditto			
110	Two pewter quart pots			
	Carried forward	445	9	3

Lot		£	s.	d.
	Brought forward	445	9	3
111	Eleven plain finger-glasses, five salts, six cruets, four tumblers, not engraved	0	7	0
112	Two dozens of port	9	10	0
113	Two ditto, more or less	4	13	0
114	One dozen of sherry, more or less	2	11	0
102A	Two decanters	1	15	0
115	The President's chair, of oak, with high back, covered with leather, with large brass studs, the top and arms carved with foliage	7	10	0

SOME OF THE MEMBERS' CHAIRS,

Copied in Oak from the Glastonbury Chair, the backs carved with the Gridiron and the Arms and Initials of each Member.

		£	s.	d.
116	J. L.—James Lonsdale	6	15	0
117	G. D.—Admiral Dundas	8	0	0
118	The Recorder—John Richards	7	15	0
119	S. M.—Stewart Marjoribanks	10	0	0
120	W. L.—William Linley	10	0	0
121	F. S. M. J. D.—The Hon. J. C. Dundas and probably Sergeant Murphy	10	5	0
122	J. C. H.—Sir John Cam Hobhouse (Lord Broughton) .	11	5	0
123	F. M.—The Hon. Fox Maule (Earl Dalhousie) . .	14	0	0
124	S.—Lord Saltoun	14	0	0
125	T. L.—Thomas Lewin	9	0	0
126	R. A. C. M.—Charles Morris	9	10	0
127	C. H.—Charles Hallett	8	10	0
128	H. M. George IV., when Prince of Wales; and H.R.H. The Duke of Sussex	20	0	0
	Carried forward	610	15	3

Lot		£	s.	d.
	Brought forward	610	15	3
129	The oak dining-table, with seven extra leaves—20 *ft.* 4 *in. long by* 4 *ft.* 7 *in. wide*, on the top is carved the President's cap, the gridiron, and a mitre	30	0	0
130	The oak sideboard, with carved back and pedestals, with carved doors—9 *ft. long*, 2 *ft.* 6 *in. deep* (not the original)	13	0	0
131	The Gridiron*	5	15	0
	Total	659	10	3

* This was not the original gridiron.

THE END.

BRADBURY, EVANS, AND CO., PRINTERS, WHITEFRIARS.